MARTIAL LAW

EARLY WARNING SERIES #1

ANGUS MCLEAN

Published 2020 by Smoking Gun Publications

ISBN 978 0 473 56089 8

ALSO BY ANGUS MCLEAN

Chase Investigations Series

Old Friends

Honey Trap

Sleeping Dogs

Tangled Webs

Dirty Deeds

Red Mist

Fallen Angel

Holy Orders

Deal Breaker

The Division Series

Smoke and Mirrors

Call to Arms

The Shadow Dancers

The Berlin Conspiracy

No Second Chance

Nicki Cooper Mystery Series

The Country Club Caper

Early Warning Series

Martial Law

Getting Home

Stand Fast

MARTIAL LAW
BY ANGUS MCLEAN

1

———

S ome would say I was paranoid, but they'd be wrong.

There's a difference between being paranoid and being smart.

To put it in real terms, if one President with a big red button and an ego problem butts heads with another with the same issues, it's probably a good time to start preparing for the worst. That's what I did, and every step of the way I prayed it would all be for nothing.

I wasn't the only one, but we were still the minority. Nobody wants their worst fears to be proved right, but I also didn't want to be one of the mindless sheeple that relied on someone else to pull their arse from the fire.

This was a country built by pioneers, tough resilient folk who travelled round the world to land on a handful of islands down near the bottom of the South Pacific. They battled adversity every step of the way, creating a national mindset of independence and humility. Shout your name from the rooftops? Expect to get cut down. Nobody round here likes a blowhard.

My name's Mark Dobson. I'm just the guy next door.

I don't care too much what people think of me, but of course there was another very good reason to keep my preparations quiet. If my predictions came true a lot of people would be caught short. Food and fuel would be the big issues. Lack of medicines. Unheated homes. Mental health issues would be exacerbated by the stress. Those that were desperate would steal to feed and clothe their families. The lowlifes would do that and more, whether they needed supplies or not. Violence would break out.

Those that were unprepared would fall victim to the predators. That wouldn't happen to my family, not on my watch.

No fucking way.

2

The chiming of my phone echoed in the steel locker as I padded across the lino floor, still wet from the shower. My leg muscles were still pinging from a hard workout – leg day was never my favourite – and I didn't make it in time.

I grabbed the phone out as it started ringing for a second time, not recognising the number on the screen.

'Dobson.'

'You free to speak?'

I didn't know the number, but it was my brother's voice. Maybe he was calling to see if I'd survived another day with our mother. Maybe he was calling to try and sell me his latest get-rich-quick idea. A month ago he'd wanted us to buy into a condo in Fiji together and make a killing on rent. Before that it had been importing high-spec cars. There was always an angle with Matt.

'I'm at the gym.'

'Is anyone listening?' His tone was urgent. 'I don't have much time.'

'Why? Are you in trouble?' If he'd been caught playing away again, I was having none of it. I'd been burned before trying to bail him out of the shit.

'No, listen, dickhead. This is fucking serious.'

I rolled my eyes even though he couldn't see me.

'And don't roll your eyes. Listen up.'

'Hurry up. I'm getting cold.'

'You've got two hours,' he said, dropping his voice. 'The PM's declaring a national state of emergency at twelve o'clock.'

My heart hit the floor. I glanced around me, but there didn't appear to be anyone within listening range. I pressed the phone hard against my ear.

'Are you serious?'

'Hundred percent. She's shitting herself and it's only a matter of time before they go full retard and declare martial law.'

'Jesus...' My voice trailed off as my mind leaped into overdrive.

'Get yourselves sorted. This is on huge lockdown. I've snuck outside for a smoke – I just hope the spooks aren't monitoring all the comms in the area, or I'm fucked. This is probably treason or something.'

Always the drama queen, but he probably wasn't far wrong.

'Watch your arse then, and get your family sorted. I'll look after Mum.'

'Shit, gotta go. The boss is calling, probably wondering where I am.'

'Thanks for the heads-up mate, I'll be in touch.' My heart was racing as the adrenaline surged through my system. 'Stay safe, bro.'

'You too. Gotta fly.'

The phone went dead and I stared at it for a moment. It was just on ten o'clock. Two hours, he'd said. I needed to move.

In two minutes I was dry and dressed, ramming my sweaty workout gear and towel into my bag. I worked the phone as I headed for the door, running through a list in my head.

A public announcement like that would cause panic. Panic led to chaos. Chaos led to trouble. I was ahead of the game right now but it wouldn't last long, so I had to be careful not blow my lead.

Gemma, Mum, Gemma's parents, her sister – they were our immediate family. Archie was at school; no issue there. My mother was at our place; no issue there either. Gemma was at work and her parents were almost two hours' away; priority. Her sister wasn't far away; secondary priority.

I hit the reception area, head down as I thumbed in a text, and I walked straight into one of the personal trainers as I went past the desk.

'Careful there, pal,' he said, putting his hand on my shoulder to stop me. He was a lean muscle-head with glamour tattoos and way too much hair product. The affect of his thick beard was diminished by the tight top he wore, deliberately showing off his nipple ring.

'Sorry mate,' I muttered, stepping around him and concentrating on my phone. I wasn't a device guy, but right now it was crucial I got this message out.

His hand stayed on my chest and he moved with me.

'Yeah, that's right...' he was saying.

I didn't have time for his chest-beating. I looked away from the phone long enough to take his hand, move it down and away and give it enough of a tweak for him to step back with a startled "Hey!"

He was still talking as I went through the doors, but it was lost in the background.

I had to move.

3

The Pak'n'Save car park was half full when I pulled up, sliding the Nissan Navara into the closest spot I could find to the doors.

I took a few seconds to try Gemma again. Still no answer. I thumbed in a quick text, hoping against hope that she would pick up and I could get her on the move to safety.

Get home now. Trust me. Do not wait.

I grabbed a trolley and headed inside, knowing with every step that the clock was ticking and the people around me had no idea what was screaming towards them. I had absolutely no doubt that most of them would be in shock when they found out. Then panic would set in and panic's best friend chaos would follow close behind.

How could I do it? How could I not put the balloon up and let them all know what was coming? Simple. It was survival, pure fucking survival in a raw form. For all I knew some of them did know already; I couldn't be the only person who got a heads-up.

That's what I told myself anyway, as I cut past the fresh produce and hit the butchery. I ignored the fresh meat in the cabinets and headed to the vacuum-packed stuff. It would last longer if I treated it right. I grabbed salami and ham and chucked it in the trolley. I moved down and found vacuum-packed beef and lamb, sticking with the red meat for its longevity and durability. More packs went into the trolley.

I headed round to the aisles, ignoring the shoppers around me. Mind on the job, no time to fuck around.

I grabbed dog biscuits and treatments, and the same for the cat. Dry goods hit the trolley in bulk –pasta, rice, rolled oats, Weetbix, some Cocoa Pops for the young fella, and dried fruit. The trolley was filling up fast. I added pasta sauces, jars and cans of the stuff.

Tinned fruit was next, all different sorts to give some variety, and some soups. The trolley was full by now and I checked my watch.

I had just under an hour and a half.

I grabbed more stuff, following a basic list in my head as I piled it high. If only it was this fast and efficient on a normal shopping day.

I hit the checkout and, being a Wednesday, was lucky enough to get in quickly. I loaded up the conveyer belt, giving the checkout operator a perfunctory nod and greeting, and waited impatiently while she scanned everything through. I bashed the plastic and also took out three hundred dollars cash, which was all she would give me.

I loaded everything into the boxes and bags in the back of the truck, locked up and tried Gemma again.

Still no answer. A big part of me wanted to just get in the tuck and barrel into town to get her. Tempting as it was, I knew I would never get back in time before the news broke and panic set in. Her work was up in the city in Freemans Bay, about fifty k's from where I stood in Pukekohe, and at this time of day I should be able to get there in three quarters of an hour or so.

The issue would be getting back. We would get stuck in there and leave my mother and our son back home without protection and only limited resources.

With my head fighting my heart, I headed back in for another round.

This time I filled the trolley with more tins of vegetables, fruit, beans, tuna and chicken, packets of crackers and biscuits, flour and sugar, tea and coffee and Milo, and powdered and UHT milk. I went

to a different checkout and raced through, taking out another couple
of hundred in cash. I knew I would be overdrawn now but that was
okay – it would soon be the least of the bank's concern.

This load went into the back of the truck as well and I returned
for a third round. As I went in the security guard at the exit gave me a
curious look, obviously noticing my strange behaviour.

'School camp,' I said as she started to approach me. 'I got
lumbered with the shopping.'

She nodded and smiled and backed away.

I went in, wondering where the hell that excuse had come from,
and loaded up for a third time. Soap, toothpaste and brushes, sham-
poo, plasters and antiseptic, sunscreen, dressings, deodorant and vita-
mins all went in the trolley. Toilet paper, wet wipes, ladies' sanitary
stuff – I got through that aisle as fast as I could, impending disaster or
not – and I was nearly done. Over an hour had gone and sweat was
running down my back.

I was gagging for a drink and something to eat. I jammed the
phone against my shoulder and rang Gemma while I grabbed stuff
from the shelves. It rang through to voicemail.

'It's me. I need you to get in your car and get home fast. Don't
question me and don't tell anyone, just go. You need to go now. This is
life and death, okay? I love you, honey. I need to know you're safe and
on the way. Call me.'

I shoved the phone back in my pocket, wondering why the hell
she wasn't answering. Likely as not she'd left her phone in the car or
in the toilet or beside the photocopier, as she often did. I had a land-
line number for her and had already tried that, but I knew that she
hot-desked at work and could be anywhere on her floor. Nobody had
answered when I called earlier.

Don't tell anyone, I'd said. That was crucial but cruel. There were
plenty of people we could tell, give them the heads-up that the shit
was about to hit the fan.

But everyone we told would tell another five, and they'd tell
another five, and so on. The slight advantage I'd been given would be
gone in seconds. All it took was one group text.

I couldn't dwell on that any longer. I loaded in muesli bars, chocolate, rubbish sacks, foil and cling wrap, bleach and disinfectants. Matches, candles, firelighters, packets of different sized batteries.

I got a third checkout operator and put that load on the credit card, taking another four hundred in cash. I manhandled the trolley outside, knowing I was getting desperately close to the deadline.

As I was loading it all into the truck I saw a car pull up nearby and a lady jump out, hurrying for the doors. I couldn't recall her name but I recognised her as the wife of a cop from Manukau. She was in a hurry and the look on her face reflected how I felt.

As she went past she glanced over and made eye contact with me. She broke her stride, saw the huge load in the back of my truck, and paused. She looked back at me and we both knew. Somehow she knew what I knew. She gave a short nod and hurried inside.

Word was getting out already.

I locked down the hatch and left the trolley on the path, getting out of there as fast as I could. I had thirty-six minutes left.

A stop at the gas station topped up the tank and my spares – petrol plus diesel for the generator at home – and I also bought the only two large containers they had for sale, filling them as well. I filled my chilly bins with bags of ice, then I grabbed a large can of energy drink from the fridge and a chunky Kit Kat, needing the sugar.

Twenty-eight minutes to go.

I took a few seconds to rip open the chocolate bar and started to neck it as I got out onto the road again. My head was spinning and I knew I needed to focus. Right now the news was pretty much contained, so I was still ahead of the game.

I pulled out, pushing my way into the traffic, and popped open the can of drink. It tasted like shit but it gave me an almost immediate boost. I could only guess what crap I was pouring into my system to get that reaction.

The last stop would be the school.

4

Gemma shouldered through the door and ran a hand over her face, trying to push away the tiredness. A one-hour phone conference with the Sydney head office had turned into nearly three hours, and she had a headache that only caffeine could cure.

Her colleagues were milling about discussing the updates from the meeting, but she had no interest in talking any more about it. She was the admin support, they were the bigwigs; that was their business. She could've got through the day just fine without even attending the meeting.

She checked her watch. Closing in on midday. She was supposed to be having lunch today with her friend Teri from Reception, but she had a backlog of work now due to the over-long meeting.

Stuff it, she thought. She had heard Brendan and Liana, the two managers of her team, planning on going out for lunch today, so fair's fair. She was about to hit the down button for the elevator when she heard Brendan's voice behind her.

'Gemma?'

She forced a smile and turned.

'You'll get the updated spreadsheet to me by one, won't you?'

'I'll try,' she said. 'I was just going to grab something to eat first.'

A frown crossed his features. 'Riiigghhtt...' He left it hanging, obviously wanting her to jump in and assure him it would all be done while he was out dining the colleague everyone knew he was either screwing now or soon would be.

Gemma let it hang and jabbed the down button. 'Enjoy your lunch,' she smiled, and stepped into the elevator. 'Dickhead,' she muttered under her breath.

Teri was on the phone when Gemma got to Reception and she leaned on the counter top, waiting. Teri waved something at her while she talked, and Gemma realised she had left her phone there earlier. Typical. At least it wasn't in the toilet this time.

She activated the screen and saw she had a screed of missed calls and messages. All from Mark. Something was obviously up. Maybe his mother had finally driven him mad and he'd killed her.

She opened up the first text message, catching Teri's eye and miming eating while she did so.

Teri nodded and pointed at the phone receiver, rolling her eyes. 'Uh-huh, yes, that's right....no...yes...'

You need to get home immediately. Don't delay. This is urgent. Call me.

Definitely mother issues. She tapped the next one.

Honey trust me this is no joke. Do not tell anyone just get in the car. Keep an ear on the news. Come home now. Don't stop. I'll see you at home.

Gemma felt a kick in her chest, a stab of worry that surprised her. This was weird. She tapped the next text, seeing it was from her mum.

We are leving soon. Dad says shud be a couple of hrs. Your hubby better nt be foolng! Luv, Mum xx.

Her Mum hadn't quite got the hang of texting, but Gemma got the message. This was no joke if her parents were involved, but what the hell was it all about?

Teri hung up the phone and turned to speak, but Gemma had already hit Mark's number and was waiting for him to pick up. She turned away from her friend, clamping the phone to her ear.

When he picked up she could hear that he was in the car.

'Oh, thank God you called.' His tone was a mix of relief and tension. 'You got my message?'

'Two of them yeah, and one from Mum. What's going on?'

She heard him swear at another motorist then exhale, gathering himself. 'I got a message from Matt. The Government are making an announcement at midday and they're going to declare a state of emergency nationwide. They may even declare martial law.'

'What the hell? Because of the earthquakes?'

'Basically, yeah. It's fucked a whole lot of things apparently. Doesn't matter why but he knows it for a fact. The power grid's in trouble and looks like it's going to crash. No power means no petrol pumps, no heating and lights; all that shit. I guess no cell phones or anything. It's nearly twelve now. You need to get in the car and get home. Are you moving?'

She looked around, seeing Teri waiting expectantly. Gemma held up a finger indicating for her to wait a minute.

'Are you serious?' she whispered into the phone.

'Dead serious. Babe, you need to go now. Stay on the line with me but grab your keys and just go, okay? Get on the road and just keep going until you get home. We'll all meet there. Are you moving?'

'Okay, okay.' Gemma felt her head swimming. She knew her husband was not one to panic, but this just seemed so surreal it was unbelievable. She knew her brother-in-law Matt was politically connected, but *really? The power grid?*

She headed back through the door, seeing Teri's puzzled look. Gemma gave her an apologetic look and pointed at her phone, pulling a face. Teri shrugged then she was out of sight as Gemma reached the elevator lobby again. The ding of an arriving car alerted Mark.

'Stay out of the lift,' he yelled down the line, 'you'll get stuck if the power goes out. Take the stairs.'

'For God's sake.' Gemma hit the stairs instead, hurrying up them awkwardly in her stupid office shoes. They weren't made for rushing, that was for sure. She heard the background noise change down the line, followed by the slamming of a car door. 'What're you doing?'

'I'm in town, grabbing some supplies,' Mark said. 'I'm going to pick up the wee man. Honey, it's like twenty minutes to go. If the phone cuts out just keep going, okay? Texts might even be able to get through. I love you and we will be okay, right?'

'Yep.' Gemma was puffing too much to talk. She passed a trio of people hurrying down the stairs and paused to look after them. They didn't look back, just kept going. 'I think the news might have broken already.'

She reached her floor and opened the fire door into the open plan office. People were milling about and there was a buzz in the air. A group of her colleagues were gathered around someone's desk, staring at the monitor.

'I think people know,' Gemma said quietly.

'You need to go,' Mark repeated urgently. 'Please honey, just get in the car and get moving before everything shuts down. Don't forget you've got your Get Home Bag if you need it.'

She was about to respond when the lights flickered and went dim. At the same time her phone crackled and she lost the connection.

There was a collective gasp around the office.

Gemma checked her phone. No signal.

Fuck it. This wasn't good.

5

T he phone was dead and the screen was telling me I had lost the signal. I tried calling her back but just got a busy signal.

I cursed and jammed the phone in my pocket as I turned towards the school. It was in a quiet side street and was normally a pain for us to get to from our place – Archie should really have been going to the local country school, but we liked this one and had been living closer to town when we had put him on the waiting list.

Right now it suited me just fine. I grabbed a slot by the entrance gate. I chugged down the last of the sugar water and wiped my mouth, planning my next move.

It struck me suddenly that maybe I was over reacting. I trusted Matt of course, but what if it wasn't going to be as bad as predicted? It wasn't unlike Government departments to have a knee jerk, but it was also standard practice for them to restrict information as well. The situation in Wellington and down-country could well be much worse than the public had been led to believe.

Earthquakes and tsunamis weren't exactly gentle. I'd seen how things had got tighter immediately after the disasters hit. The Canterbury earthquakes back in 2012 had been bad enough, but this was all that and more.

No, this was not an over-reaction on my part. Clearly we couldn't rely on the Government to bail us out. This was about survival, and family came first.

The office lady was on the phone when I entered the foyer, and as I signed in to the Visitor's Book I heard her muttering something to herself about the phones playing up. She put the receiver down as I was scarpering for the door.

'All okay, Mark?' she called out.

I stopped with the door open and gave her a wave. 'Just grabbing Archie for a doctor's appointment,' I said. I didn't wait for a response but headed straight for his classroom. The kids were all in their reading groups when I came in the side door, and several heads turned my way.

I gave Archie a smile and a thumbs-up as I approached. He grinned quickly then put his finger to his lips to shush me. Seven years old and already giving orders. He made a show of concentrating on his book as one of the other kids read a line.

The teacher paused to turn to me.

'Sorry,' I said, 'I just need to grab Archie. I forgot he's got an appointment.'

She frowned to make sure I understood I was inconveniencing her. 'I see, right. What kind of appointment?'

'A personal one.' I set my jaw firmly.

I had no doubt that the staff knew of my history, and there were all sorts of rumours and lies that had been spread. She probably thought I was some kind of psycho, ready to explode at any moment. Hopefully it was enough to encourage her to leave it alone.

Archie jumped up and grabbed his book bag, quickly putting his book away while I waited. That done, he came over and I knelt down so he could give me a big hug. I felt a lump in my throat as I held my son against my chest.

'He'll be coming straight back?' the teacher asked.

'Yep,' I said, lying through my teeth. 'Come on bud, let's get a wriggle on.'

I led him outside to the cubbyholes where they kept their bags. While he put his book bag away, I looked back at the kids inside. So young and innocent, quietly reading away with their teachers –apart from the two boys who were flicking bogies at each other, and the ADHD girl who was jumping around looking for attention while her teacher aide was distracted by someone else – they had no idea what was going on.

I spotted a couple of Archie's little mates at one of the tables. One of them waved and I waved back. My heart lurched. Was I doing the right thing by not giving them all a heads-up? The school had an emergency procedure where parents all got a text to notify them of an event. I could go to the office and let them know to send out an alert.

I checked my watch. Twelve minutes to go. It wouldn't make any difference now; they'd all know soon enough, if they didn't already. Gemma's workmates did, so it was safe to assume the news had leaked.

Archie had put on his sandals and was wrestling with his jacket. I helped him sort out his sleeves and went to zip him up, but he stepped away.

'No Dad, leave it open.'

Of course. My jacket was unzipped, so he wanted his the same way. When I wore a cap, he wore a cap. If I wore shorts, he wore shorts. I got that.

'Grab your bag, buddy,' I said.

'Aren't I coming back for lunch?'

'No, we're going home.'

'Why?' He was curious but not curious enough not to follow instructions. He slung his Lightning McQueen bag onto his back.

'We've just got some things to do at home with Grandma.'

'But you said I had an appointment.' He was definitely confused now, trying to get his head around it all. 'Am I going to the doctors, Dad?'

He was holding my hand as we walked to the truck. I stroked his knuckles with my thumb.

'No buddy, not the doctors. But we need to get home.' I bleeped the locks and took his bag while he climbed up into his car seat. 'You know how the earthquakes happened, and there's lots of flooding down in Wellington and around there?'

He nodded. We had discussed it all at home, and I knew they'd done some work on it at school.

'Well that's all caused some problems, so the Prime Minister – the lady that runs the country – is telling everyone that there's a big emergency. So what that means for us is that the supermarkets and shops aren't going to have much food and stuff, and the schools will close for a bit while everything gets sorted out.' I had eye to eye with him. 'Does that make sense?'

'But Dad, it's not school holidays yet.' He scratched his knee while he turned the news over in his head. 'What about reading? I didn't finish my book today.'

'That's okay,' I said, 'we've got your book and you can read it to me or Grandma this afternoon. And we've got lots of books at home.'

Archie nodded innocently. 'And I can get Grandma to read with me.'

'That's right.' I leaned in and kissed his soft cheek. 'Grandma loves reading to you, doesn't she?'

I got in and fired it up while Archie carried on chatting away. I loved listening to his little stories but my mind was elsewhere just now. It was coming up on midday. I flicked the radio on as we drove away from school.

Instead of ads playing as normal there was a very serious sounding DJ, telling me that there was about to be an important announcement from the Prime Minister and they were going across live to the temporary Parliament.

I turned onto the main road, hearing the Prime Minister's voice over the speakers.

'...it is with regret that I must declare a national state of emergency effective immediately...'

It sounded like she was almost drowned out by shouted questions and it took a few seconds for calm to be restored.

'I encourage all members of our communities to remain calm and ensure that loved ones and neighbours are secure and taken care of. Civil Defence and all the emergency services are working hard, round the clock, to ensure that this situation is dealt with as soon as possible. To assist them in that I have mobilised the armed forces, so you can expect to see Army, Navy and Air Force personnel deploying in the communities to help those that need help. They will also be assisting Police to maintain the peace.'

It sounded like a step short of martial law to me.

She droned on with some spin which frustrated me. I wanted some specifics but she said that it was difficult to put a time frame on the emergency at this stage. It was therefore difficult to predict the level of impact the emergency would have on food supplies and whether there would be fuel shortages or not.

It sounded to me like a decision had been made, but without much forethought about the impact that decision would have. Or if there had been, the conclusions weren't being shared with the general public; including the minority of taxpayers that had put that bunch of muppets in power.

The announcement finished with the reminder to listen out for further information, and to comply with instructions from the authorities as everyone worked together to get the situation under control.

It didn't fill me with confidence. I switched the radio off.

As far as I was concerned, it was up to us to look after ourselves.

6

Sandy McMasters added a pile of clothes to her open suitcase and looked across the bed at her husband. 'Are you really sure about this?' she said.

Rob stopped cramming in socks and underwear and straightened up. His suitcase was smaller than his wife's and nearly full. 'Well I'm not happy about it, if that's what you mean,' he said. 'But Mark's no panicker – in fact, he's the complete opposite of that – so I trust his judgement. If he says it's time to move, then it's time to move.'

'Hmmm.' Sandy paused, a nicely folded merino jumper in her hands. 'It just...I don't know.'

'Honey, I know what you're thinking.' Rob looked her in the eye. 'This is way out of left field, and neither of us wants to pack up and go stay with Gem and Mark, but hopefully it will only be a few days and it'll all blow over.' He smiled, his blue eyes twinkling. 'Believe me, after nearly fifty years, I know what you're thinking.'

Sandy felt herself smile despite her misgivings and added the merino jumper to her case. 'Hopefully. At least we'll get to spend a few days with wee Archie. He'll be on you like Poppa's little shadow.'

Rob grinned, knowing she was right. His grandson was the apple of his eye and the feeling was mutual. Having raised daughters, Rob was particularly taken with his youngest grandchild, and having the boy's middle name named after him was something he cherished.

He turned to the wardrobe and took a pair of jeans and a pair of cargo pants off their hangars, folded them carefully and placed them in the suitcase. He was almost done. The contents of his suitcase were meticulously neat – the habits instilled by the Navy during his youth were far from dying off. He burrowed into the back of the wardrobe, pushing aside the long coats, and emerged with a dusty rifle in his hands.

'Is that thing still here?' Sandy cocked an eyebrow as he leaned the rifle against the side of the bed. 'I thought you gave that to Mark?'

'Never quite got round to it.' Rob found the bolt in his bedside table drawer and fitted it to the rifle. He picked the weapon up and grinned. 'That's a Lee-Enfield No. 1 Mk IV, dear – the pride of the Navy.'

'And what exactly are you doing with it, anyway?' she inquired. 'Shouldn't it be in a museum somewhere?'

Rob sidestepped the question, digging around in the back of his drawer again. He produced a small oilskin bag and from that he removed two charger clips, each loaded with five rounds.

'I wonder if Mark's still got some .303,' he mused, as he gave the ammo a wipe with a small cleaning cloth.

'Shouldn't all that be in a safe?' Sandy persisted.

'Probably,' he agreed, giving the rifle a wipe with the cloth as well. 'I should probably have a license too.'

Sandy shook her head at her husband's misdemeanours; he'd always been an irascible type, and it was typical of him to do this. She decided it was best not to pursue it just now and carried on with her packing. She knew, and he knew too, that that wasn't necessarily the end of the matter though.

By the time their suitcases were packed and waiting by the door it was more than an hour since Mark's message had come through. Rob put the jug on and made a cup of tea while Sandy set about filling the chilly bin from the garage. She filled it with the perishables from the fridge, knowing they would not last too long. The last thing she wanted to do when this blew over in a few days was to come home to curdled milk and wilted fruit and vegetables.

She eased herself into a chair at the dining room table and accepted the cup of tea her husband passed over. Her mind was racing and it seemed like it had been a long day already. She still wasn't quite sure what to make of the situation – sure, things were bad down south, but that couldn't affect the whole country could it? And even if it upset things to some extent, surely things would blow over in a few days and everything would return to normal?

Things like this didn't happen in their little part of the world. Waihi Beach was a coastal paradise, certainly not home to riots and looting and civil unrest. Not that anyone had specifically said that, but she had the impression that was what her son-in-law was thinking. He'd always been serious when it came to things like this, his policing and the like. She had no doubt that was why he had ended up in the position he had; it was not in his nature to back down to people trying to threaten him or his family.

He had gone from being a dedicated Police Sergeant, putting in extra hours to catch bad guys, to being turfed out. He had weathered many things over his years in uniform but one bad decision had cost him dearly. A gang member with a chip on his shoulder had pushed his luck – and Mark's patience – too far. The gang member had lost some teeth and Mark had lost his job. Even though the work he did now as a private eye and security consultant paid well, she knew his heart wasn't in it. He had told her once that he would always regret his decision that day; he had been wrong and he had paid a hell of a price.

But if he was right about the current situation then maybe he was the right person to be around.

She took a sip. 'When do you want to leave?' she asked, putting her cup down.

'As soon as we're done here,' Rob replied. He took a mouthful of tea, swallowed, and sucked his teeth. He looked pensive. 'I think the sooner we get going the better, my girl.'

Sandy smiled inwardly at his use of her pet name. 'Have you got enough pills?' she asked. 'Do you think we should stop at the pharmacy on the way?' Like her, he took pills daily for his cholesterol.

Rob gave a slow nod. 'Probably. I've got a couple of weeks' worth, but just in case, I guess. What about you?'

'I just filled mine the other day. I've got another repeat waiting though, so maybe I should just get that filled anyway.'

'Righto then.' Rob drained his cup and got to his feet. 'I'll put these bags in the bus.'

'Oh.' Sandy gave him a look of surprise. 'You don't want to take the car?'

'No.' He shook his head firmly, his mind made up. 'We'll take the bus. Young Archie loves the bus.'

The bus was their most recent acquisition, a 4-berth Mercedes motorhome. It had only done a few miles in the time they'd had it but they planned to do plenty more. Always the more sociable of the two, Rob had signed them up for a motorhome group and they had taken "the bus" on the first tour just a month ago, stopping at Gemma and Mark's for a night on the way home.

Archie had been allowed to sleep the night in the campervan and had talked about it for days afterwards. Sandy knew that that alone was reason enough for Rob to take the bus this time.

She watched him head off towards the door, an overnight bag and the old rifle in his hands. She looked out the window towards the flower garden she had lovingly created and tended to. It was a blaze of colour as it always was, whatever the season. Beyond it was Rob's vegetable garden and his fruit trees, where he spent so many hours of his days, pottering. They were happy in this little paradise, living the retired life.

Sandy stood and picked up her empty tea cup. She hoped they would be back here soon when things settled down.

7

Rural living had distinct pluses and minuses. The minuses were having no shops handy, everywhere being a car ride, and spotty service from the utility companies. The pluses were having space and fresh air and neighbours I couldn't hit with a stone.

Turning off State Highway 1 onto State 2 put the Bombay Hills to my left. State 2 headed over to the Coromandel and Bay of Plenty on the east coast. We were now officially out of Auckland and in the north Waikato.

I ducked off the highway onto a side road and after a couple of minutes of meandering past farms we reached our own road. It was a long no exit road and we were roughly half-way down. I turned the truck into our entranceway, juddered over the cattle stop and headed up the driveway of dirt and loose metal. Our property included the paddocks to both sides of the drive and the house was about two thirds of the way back to the rear of our land.

A shelter belt of trees to the left of the house marked the boundary on that side, and a gully dropping away to the right was the other marker. The driveway ran down the middle of the front two paddocks to a parking area between the garage and the shed that was going to become a sleepout in due course, and an implement shed further down the track behind the house.

The house was a basic weatherboard farmhouse with a good-sized deck at the front and a private outdoor dining area at the back. The attached double garage was adjacent to the driveway.

The 200-hectare dairy farm to the south was home to the Macklin family and to the north was a row of lifestyle blocks similar to ours. Across the road from us was an older Dutch couple, the van Dijks. They leased out most of their farm for dry stock but stayed on the land simply for the lifestyle. They kept bees and made cheese which they took to markets.

I pulled up beside the garage and killed the engine. My Mum was at the front door by the time I'd got out, her cell phone in her hand and a worried expression on her face.

'I can't quite believe it,' she said, fidgeting nervously with the phone. 'Have you heard anything else from Matthew? I can't get through on the phone and they're just repeating the same thing over and over on the radio.'

Her face lit up when Archie made a dash for her with his arms out. She bent and hugged him, unable to get down and pick him up anymore. He broke away and headed inside with his school bag hanging from one arm and his drink bottle clutched in the other hand, looking for either biscuits or the dog or both.

I gave my Mum a hug and she hung onto me. 'It's going to be okay,' I said, maybe more in hope than certainty. I broke the embrace and held her by the shoulders. 'Yeah?'

Her eyes were wet but she nodded. 'I hope so,' she said, wiping her eyes with the back of her hand. 'I'm worried about Matthew and the kids and everyone.'

I noticed that she mentioned my brother and the kids but not his wife, Michelle. She'd never been good with daughters-in-law, which had caused problems in the family for years. I let it go for now; I was worried too.

'I got hold of Gem,' I said, knowing she probably wouldn't ask. 'She's on the way home now hopefully.'

'That's good.' I may have imagined it, but there was some trace of genuineness there.

'And Rob and Sandy are hopefully on the way too.'

She nodded but said nothing to that. Again, issues there. As far as she could see the McMasters' had too much influence in our lives.

Jethro bounded up then, fresh from adventures in the paddock. He was a three-year-old Border Collie with boundless energy and a passion for chasing rabbits. He was Archie's best pal, so brushed past us and went looking for him.

I tasked my mother with sorting Archie out for lunch while I lugged all my purchases inside. It took so many trips that they were finished eating – although Mum hardly seemed to have touched her sandwich – by the time I had finished.

I stashed what I could in the kitchen and the rest went into the garage. The normal emergency supplies we had were stored in a 2-door cupboard, most of the shelves filled with enough food to feed us for a fortnight. Stacked beside and on top of it were plastic storage bins and old paint pails that had been cleaned up, all containing medical gear, batteries, and other bits and pieces.

I filled the cupboard shelves then sorted out the chilly bins with ice and put the cold stuff that hadn't fit in the fridge into them. The spare bags of ice went into the chest freezer for use later on. I emptied a couple more storage bins of other junk and filled them with food as well.

I was sweating and parched by the time I finished, but I was satisfied with what I had achieved. Surveying the preparations, I wondered how long the food would last. Even with no crystal ball at hand I still suspected it would not be long enough.

I returned to the house and emptied a large glass of water, refilled it and took that down too. Archie had tagged Grandma to read, so she was working through a Star Wars book with him. It had been a long time since she'd played in the sandpit with Luke, Leia and the gang, but she was giving it a fair effort.

I left them to it and made myself a quick cheese and Vegemite sandwich. I stood at the kitchen bench and started making lists while I ate.

The first list was of people I needed to contact; most of that was complete. The second list was of things I still needed to obtain; it was a speculative list, considering I had no idea how long this state of emergency would last. At least a few weeks was my absolute best guess, in which case we would be sound with what we had. But if the grid went down and/or martial law was declared, then who knew? Could be months.

The large vegetable gardens on our property gave us fresh produce in every season, as did the fruit trees and berries. We had chooks that gave us eggs, a sow that cleaned up food scraps and kept us in pork, and a couple of beefies that were destined for the freezer.

We had bore water in addition to the standard tank water, plus extra tank water from the gutters which we used for watering the garden. The property was a five-acre block carved off from a neighbouring farm when the old boy passed on and his family downsized and cashed up.

We had solar panels and a fireplace to keep the power bills down. The portable generator could run the fridge or freezer, or power the lights if needs be. I planned to use that just enough to keep food fresh rather than light the house.

Being out in the sticks meant we had the usual native visitors to the property, and it was regular sport to deal with the rabbits, rats and possums. Jethro and the cat, Pepper, helped to keep the wildlife under control too. A local woman had a business making blankets, socks, scarves and beanies from possum fur, and took all she could get from us. We did it on a barter system so had supplies of some of her products, and I'd never had warmer feet in winter.

We were sufficiently equipped here to survive off the land for quite some time, but exactly how long depended on the conditions and how many people we would be helping. Presuming Gemma and her parents got here, that gave us five adults and a child, plus the animals. My father was dead and there was nobody else in my family

I would reasonably expect to turn up. Gemma's sister and her family might do, and although I had contacted them, I hadn't heard back.

What if neighbours came knocking, asking for food or supplies? Friends or workmates? Strangers in need? All bridges that would have to be crossed when we got to them but to my mind, the bottom line was that family came first.

If it turned out to be an emergency that lasted some time and resulted in the type of lawlessness that would go with that, a la Hurricane Katrina in New Orleans, then things would get hairy. There would be insufficient law enforcement around to help, and when people get hungry and desperate, or just when they have nothing to stop them, they revert to savagery pretty damn fast.

And we needed to be prepared for that.

8

_____

With that in mind I headed down the hallway to the spare bedroom, where the gun safe was concealed in the wardrobe. Grandma was currently using the room and she had hung some clothes in the wardrobe.

I had never been a big gun-nut, but I recognised the need for tools. I legally possessed three firearms for sporting use, and I took them all out, leaning them against the wall.

There was a lever action Rossi Puma in .357 Magnum, a pump action 12-gauge Mossberg 500, and a semi-automatic Ruger 10/22. Each weapon had a sling, the Mossberg's barrel was Magnaported to reduce the kick, and the Rossi and Ruger each had a basic 3-9x scope. The Ruger also had a suppressor. I had a decent supply of ammo for each weapon, along with extra bits of kit.

When the Government changed the gun laws following the Christchurch terror attack, the affect on lawful gun owners had been immense. The gangs hadn't given a shit and carried on as normal. Many lawful owners handed in the guns they had legally purchased but which were now outlawed.

Many others, including yours truly, hadn't. The problem with having no national gun register was that the Government had no way of knowing exactly what weapons a normal A-Category license holder possessed.

My plans to go bigger and better were thwarted by two things; disapproval from the wife and finances. It would've been great to have a decent semi-auto rifle but I couldn't justify the expense, nor could I weather the storm indoors. I'd done enough to nearly derail my marriage without pushing the envelope too far. I would have to make do with what I had.

Besides, the best way to survive a battle was to avoid the battle in the first place. I was confident that I was skilled enough with what I had to outgun most comers. A military unit would be a different story of course, and if someone opened up on me with an M60, well, I'd be running like hell.

As things were turning out, I was glad of what I had.

I loaded the Rossi and put it aside. I took an Army-surplus webbing belt from the wardrobe and filled two of the ammo pouches with .357 Magnum rounds. I put it beside the lever action rifle and opened another box to load the Mossberg, leaving the chamber empty. It had a 20-inch barrel and with 3-inch shells, it took seven rounds plus one up the spout. I made sure the buttstock sleeve was full with another six rounds, and put the shotgun aside as well. The ammo bandolier for it was already full.

I left the Ruger for now and put all three weapons back in the safe, locking it again and tucking the key into its hiding place. I didn't anticipate needing the weapons just yet, and didn't want to scare anyone any more than necessary.

I headed outside again, making my way to the sleepout attached to the garage. It had previously been used as a bedroom and had a small en-suite. We had used it for storage and occasionally for guests, but it would need some work for it to be used permanently in that capacity.

I opened the windows and door to air it, grabbed a spade from the garage and ducked around the back of the building. There was an old

water trough there that was no longer used. I shifted it aside and dug
into the dirt. I soon scraped something hard and it took another
minute to dig out a metal ammo can wrapped in an oilskin bag. I
filled in the hole and moved the trough back into place.

Putting aside the spade, I removed the can from the bag and
opened it. Originally home to a thousand rounds of 5.56mm military
ammo, it now contained a holstered pistol and three magazines.

The firearms inside the house were what I legally possessed and
they had all been checked by a vetting officer. However, since I was
waiting for my licence to be upgraded to include a B-Category
endorsement that would me to possess pistols, I had been forced to
make other arrangements.

The fact that I was stood down from duty – suspended, but the
department doesn't like to call it that – while I awaited trial on an
assault charge, my application had been put on hold. They reviewed
my suitability to even possess firearms at all, and it took legal inter-
vention to keep my licence.

Even though the case was over and I had been cleared, the
department had decided to stick it to me and keep my application on
hold for two years. Those two years were nearly up, but I hadn't
waited around.

A visit to the Police shooting range at Penrose to catch up with an
old buddy had given me the opportunity to slip into the strong room.

In addition to the racks of Bushmaster M4 carbines and Glock 17
sidearms they kept a few odds and sods for training purposes. It
would even have been easy enough to swipe one of the Glocks, but I
knew that the training weapons got thrashed and were often barely
holding together. Not only that but it would also be noticed pretty
quick, what with two training sessions each day going through the
range.

While Wally was on the phone I had ducked down the hall
through the cleaning/briefing room and through the open door to the
strong room. At the back left was a small row of hooks with the odds
and sods. Most were old air pistols or homemade jobs that had been
seized, but there were a few serviceable weapons.

There was a single semi auto, being a blued Browning High Power. That went straight into the deep pocket of my jacket along with the three magazines on the shelf above it. I had wanted more and the several revolvers of various configurations were tempting, but I knew that Wally wouldn't be long. Within ten seconds of entering the room I was out again.

That had been six months ago and I'd heard nothing further about it, even from Wally, although he knew me well enough to have had his suspicions. The department doesn't like to admit mistakes, and missing firearms is pretty up there. I doubted that the bosses even knew about it.

The pistol had remained buried at home, coming out only a few times for a shoot up. I'd sourced 9mm Parabellum rounds for it even though I didn't own a 9mm weapon. I simply told the gun store guy that I was buying them as a present for a mate who was a pistol shooter, and took possession of some bricks of quality 124 grain +Ps.

I had sourced two Safariland holsters online; a black nylon pancake holster and a black thigh rig. I also got a double magazine pouch for the Browning magazines.

I returned the spade to the garage and left the oilskin bag and ammo tin on the workbench. I took the weapon and accessories inside to the gun safe.

I filled the magazines and slipped two into the mag pouch, loaded the third into the Browning and applied the safety, leaving the chamber empty. With the pistol safely stashed under lock and key I went back out to the lounge, where Grandma and Archie were still engaged with the Star Wars gang. Grandma was a bit lost with some of the names but Archie was always keen to help.

I leaned in the doorway and watched them for a while, getting that warm glow that parents get from their child's pleasure. With the sun coming in the big windows and the animals in the green pastures beyond, a grandmother reading with a wee boy, on any other day it would have been an idyllic scene.

I felt my chest constrict as I was reminded for the millionth time in the last few hours that today was not just another day. Today was the day that things changed, probably forever. Having an interest in such things, I had followed events like Hurricane Katrina and the Christchurch earthquakes. I knew that it often took years for people to recover from such events, and some never did.

It left one over-riding question on my mind.

How the fuck was I going to keep my family safe?

9

The pharmacist had wanted to talk as she always did, but Rob had managed to keep the show moving and get them out of there without too much of a delay. He knew there was a state of emergency declared and he didn't need to discuss it with the pharmacist.

Sandy had wanted to make lunch to take with them but he had dug his toes in and pushed her to hurry up, offering to shout her lunch on the way. Never one to miss out on that rare opportunity, she had put her bag in the bus and saddled up.

Outside the summer holiday period Waihi Beach town was never exactly bustling, but there was a regular flow of activity as people came and went, walking and driving and cycling. While Rob popped into the pharmacy, Sandy went to the bakery and picked up a cheese and bacon-topped loaf and a couple of coffees for the road. They stopped at the ATM and each withdrew the maximum they could from each card, including their credit cards. Who knew what was going to happen in the next while, and having cash on hand was always a good idea.

Both of them noticed that town was busier than normal and there was a definite sense of urgency in the air. The Four Square supermarket was humming and the GAS station had a queue down the road.

They went on by and made good time through Waihi and the winding, narrow Karangahake Gorge, seeing no signs of general panic on the roads. Even most of the usual roadside fruit and vege stalls were in place. The radio was tuned to a talkback station which featured regular news bulletins. There was plenty of discussion about the state of emergency, but nothing of substance. Sandy tuned out and she knew that Rob would have done too – unless it was to do with rugby, racing, or politics he had no interest.

They got to Paeroa, the first town on the other side of the gorge, and Rob joined the queue at a Gull. He noticed that the tall electronic price sign was off so it was anyone's guess what they were charging. They waited for fifteen minutes to get to a bowser, during which time several cars left without getting gas.

Getting out, Rob found a handwritten sign taped to the bowser.

CASH ONLY. PAY INSIDE. PUMPS LOCKED.

He binned the empty coffee cups and joined the next queue inside. There were two Indian guys behind the counter, processing sales. One was arguing with a punter who wanted to pay by card.

'No EFTPOS,' the attendant was saying, 'cash only.'

'Dude, I've got my gas here every week for four years and you're turning me away?' The motorist was getting red in the face and Rob could hear the stress in his voice.

'Sorry sir, is cash only. Management rules.'

'For fuck's sake, this is bullshit! Is your EFTPOS system not working or something?'

'Sorry sir, is cash only. Next please.'

'Fuckin' wanker.' The motorist turned away and slapped a display of chocolate bars off the counter onto the floor.

'Don't do that sir, please,' the attendant said, his monotone not even flickering. 'Next please.'

'Fuck you, ya curry-munching homo.' The motorist kicked over a stand of cheap sunglasses on the way to the door. 'I'll be back.'

Rob kept an eye on him as he left. The guy was just an average looking white guy in his thirties, the sort you would pass in the street and not give a second glance. The behaviour he had just exhibited was far from normal, and Rob figured that, if this was how quickly things deteriorated when the pressure came on, he and Sandy wanted to be off the streets sharpish.

He reached the counter and got out his wallet, thankful that he had always been a believer in paying cash.

'How much is your 91?' he said.

'Is on the sign, sir.' Rather than answering the question, the attendant pointed to another handwritten sign on the counter, listing the fuel prices.

Rob felt his eyebrows shoot up to his fringe when he saw the prices. Somehow the price of unleaded gas had more than in the last couple of hours. He looked at the attendant.

'Taking advantage of the current situation?' he said.

The attendant looked at him flatly. 'Is another gas station down the road, sir.'

Rob shook his head, feeling a twinge of sympathy for the angry man who'd just left. He counted out several notes.

'I can't just fill it then and pay after?'

'No sir.'

'Come on mate,' said someone in the queue behind him. 'I haven't got all day.'

Rob ignored him. 'I'll take forty litres,' he said.

He paid over the cash, checked his change and hurried out to the bowser. The forecourt was completely full and cars waited out on the road. He filled the ten-litre jerry can he kept as a spare and pumped the rest into the tank. He was almost finished when the pump stopped working. At the same time the lights on the forecourt and in the shop went out.

Checking out on the street he could see that the café across the road was also in darkness. Other motorists at the pumps were waving at the attendants in the shop, and someone yelled at them to turn the bowsers back on.

'That ain't gunna happen,' Rob muttered to himself.

He hung up the pump and secured the jerry can in the storage locker under the cabin. He had the feeling things were about to turn to rat shit, but the only surprise was how quickly that happened.

By the time he'd climbed into the cab and was buckling up, angry motorists were berating the attendants. Rob spotted the guy who'd been turned away come trotting back across the forecourt with a tyre iron in his hand. He went straight to the night-pay window beside the counter and belted it, cracking it with his second strike.

'Best we get moving, my girl,' Rob said. He released the handbrake and slipped the motorhome into gear.

Someone else grabbed a car battery from a display at the shop doors and hurled it through the glass with an almighty crash.

Sandy let out a gasp of shock and Rob saw someone jump the counter inside and throw a punch at one of the attendants.

He goosed the accelerator and got the hell out of there. Pandemonium was really breaking out behind them as they hit the main drag and hung a right.

'Should we call the Police?' Sandy said, digging in her handbag for her phone.

'If you want to,' Rob said. 'Doubt you'll get through though, they're probably overloaded already.'

'No signal.'

'Let's just keep our heads down and get to the kids' place.' Rob locked the doors and focussed on the road ahead. The Lee Enfield was tucked in behind the front seat in case he needed it, but hopefully it wouldn't come to that.

They got through town with no further dramas and headed north on State Highway 2, the next stop being Ngatea, twenty minutes away.

10

The office had taken on a weird vibe, with people milling about and talking in hushed tones. Nobody really seemed to know what to do, and Gemma noticed that there was an absence of managers.

She went to her desk and sat down, her head starting to spin. It seemed surreal. It was like being a spectator to something big but not actually being involved. The reality was quickly sinking in and Gemma knew that Mark was right. She needed to get moving.

Home was a long way from the city, and traffic was bad enough at normal times. Decision made, she reached under the desk for her belongings. She put her handbag to one side and kicked off her work shoes. She was lacing up her Asics trainers when she sensed someone beside her.

It was her supervisor, Leoni, giving her a quizzical look. 'What're you doing?' she said.

Gemma finished lacing and straightened up. 'Getting my shoes on,' she replied.

Leoni frowned, obviously not sure how to proceed. She was a nice girl, but in Gemma's opinion, she lacked bite. She had no issue with organising herself but was too flighty to be a good leader.

'Where's the boss?' Gemma asked, sliding open her top desk drawer.

'I don't know.' Leoni looked around, not seeing anyone higher up the food chain than herself. 'I better find someone...'

Gemma let her go do that and took a few moments to grab some bits and pieces from her desk; car keys, phone charger, drink bottle and lunchbox. Looking around the office, she realised nobody else was moving. Most were still in the same huddle as when she'd walked in, and nobody was taking any notice of her.

She stood, crammed her bits and pieces into her handbag, and headed for the door. As she went through she could hear Leoni calling for everyone's attention behind her. Gemma ignored the call and kept going, taking the stairs down.

As she passed each floor she could see all the other offices were in a similar disorganised state to her own. The odd person joined her on the stairs, all looking worried, but nobody spoke. There was a definite sense of urgency in the air.

She pushed through the fire door at the B1 level of the basement, pausing to hold the door when she heard feet hurrying down the stairs behind her.

'Thanks.' It was Alex Parker from IT, a thin young guy with floppy dark hair and a long nose.

'Going home?' Gemma said as she started towards her car.

'Definitely.' He nodded his head vigorously. 'My Mum'll freak out when she hears the news.'

Gemma nodded to herself, wondering momentarily how her own parents had taken the news. Her Dad was a tough old rooster but they were both elderly now, and her Mum had always been a softie. He was the one who would kick a ball around with Archie and she was the one who fussed over him when he hurt himself.

She pushed the thought aside, just hoping that they reached home safely. She knew that if they were with Mark they would be safe. If her Dad was a tough old rooster then Mark was his younger self, maybe harder. Definitely hardnosed, to the point that it got him in trouble. But above all else he was super-protective of his family.

She bleeped the locks on the Galant as she approached. The paint was faded and it was nearly twenty years old, but it was serviced regularly and ran well. She popped the boot and lifted the lid. The boot was home to various bits of crap – reusable grocery bags, a soccer ball, an old cat cage she'd been meaning to drop off to the charity store.

And a black High Sierra day pack.

Gemma dropped her handbag on the floor of the boot and grabbed the black pack. Mark called it a Get Home Bag, and she knew it was tailored for her. It contained enough gear and supplies for 24 hours, the idea being that if she broke down or was otherwise stranded somewhere she should be able to get home within that time.

Somehow, she doubted that the AA would be of much use today.

She opened the bag up and checked inside. It looked untouched since Mark had gone through it with her several months ago. She secured it and closed the boot. The Galant started easily and she turned the volume down on the stereo, flicking it over from CD to the radio. Now was the time for news, not Pink.

The classic hits station was all static. Gemma reversed out of the slot and moved towards the exit ramp up to the street. She switched stations as she drove, getting nothing but static on another Top 40 frequency. She pulled up behind another car waiting to get out, a little green hatchback with an anti-mining sticker in the rear window. She recognised Alex's profile as he leaned out the window to swipe his access card to open the roller gate.

Gemma waited impatiently while he fannied about, flicking to a talkback station she knew Mark sometimes listened to. The announcer's voice came through clear enough.

'...and to check on family and neighbours. The Civil Defence department has been mobilised and Civil Defence posts will be open to assist those that need help. Please do not make voice calls on your phone as this will overload the networks and they need to remain open for emergency services' use. If you need to contact people you are advised to send a text...'

Alex was still mucking round with his access card and Gemma pulled on the handbrake before getting out of the car.

'What's wrong?' she called out.

'It's not working.'

Gemma strode over and swiped her own card in front of the reader. Nothing. She noticed the red LED light was on but had only a dull glow.

'The power must be out,' Alex said, 'or close to it.'

Gemma noticed for the first time that the overhead lights were barely glowing. Other cars were pulling up behind them and someone honked their horn. Gemma shot a look in that direction and swiped her card again. Still nothing.

She walked back towards her car. 'The gate's not opening,' she called out to the driver behind her car, a woman she recognised from Marketing. 'The power must be out.'

The woman cursed and slapped her steering wheel in frustration. A guy got out of a vehicle a couple back and strode forward, big arms swinging round a big belly. Gemma recognised him as Nick Some-body-or-other from Sales. He was loud and brash and referred to himself as Big Nick. Gemma knew that the nickname had been bastardised behind his back to Big Dick.

'So it's not working,' he said, producing his own swipe card. He waded past her and thrust his card against the reader, as if he was about to prove the silly girl wrong and magically open the gate because he had a penis. Nothing. He tried tapping it, but still nothing.

Big Nick straightened up, giving a harrumph. Gemma arched an eyebrow at him.

'Didn't it work?' she said.

Big Nick scowled and gestured for everyone to move back, waving his hands like an air traffic controller. 'Everyone back up,' he shouted. 'I'll bring the Battle Truck up.'

Gemma rolled her eyes. 'What're you going to do?' she said.

'I'm going to smash the fuckin' thing down.'

Gemma shrugged to herself and got in her car. Despite his

bravado, she had to admit he had a point. They needed to get out of the basement somehow.

Once the other cars had cleared a path, Big Nick moved forward in his Battle Truck. Gemma noticed that it wasn't really a battle truck of any sort, but rather some kind of sporty family-style SUV with tinted windows and all the gadgets. She doubted it had ever even felt mud under its tyres; just another Remuera tractor.

He edged up to the roller and nudged it with the pristine bumper. The roller gate rattled and wobbled. He pushed harder, then backed up and leaped forward, hitting the roller with a loud crash. It bent and buckled.

Gemma watched as he took another run, flinching involuntarily as he smashed into it and ripped the roller away from one side. It half folded over the front of his Battle Truck and got stuck as he backed up for another shot at it. There was a loud screeching and tearing sound and the Battle Truck shuddered to a halt.

Big Nick jumped out, cursing and swearing as he tried to wrench the buckled gate from beneath his bumper. Somebody honked their horn and he sent a verbal burst their way too, before getting back behind the wheel, revving the engine and shooting backwards. He hit the front of Alex's hatchback with a crunch and sent it backwards into the car behind him, which was the Marketing woman.

The Marketing woman – Amanda, maybe? – jumped out, shrieking at Big Nick and flapping her arms as she surveyed the damage to her shiny white Audi. Big Nick ignored her and gunned it forward again, tearing the roller gate away from its moorings with a piercing screech of tortured metal. For a moment it looked like he'd done it, then the Battle Truck ground to a halt again with the crushed roller wrapped around its wheels and axle.

'Faaark!' Big Nick alighted again, kicking furiously at the wrecked gate as other workers began to get out of their cars.

Sitting off to the side, Gemma could see that his truck was completely blocking the exit and was going nowhere. Her heart sank as she realised there was no way that any of them would be getting out of the basement in a hurry.

Alex was standing by his car, staring forlornly at the crumpled bonnet. The basement was becoming clogged with exhaust fumes and people were getting vocal and agitated.

Gemma turned the Galant off and got out. She checked her phone and saw it had no service, which wasn't unusual down in the basement garage.

Big Nick was in a shouting match with Amanda from Marketing now, both of them going to town about the other's stupidity. Another guy piped up and tried to settle them both down, and got a double serve of vitriol for his troubles. Someone else honked their horn and Big Nick turned on him, threatening to "yank that fuckin' horn out and shove it up your fuckin' arse, you fuckin' pencil-neck fuck."

Gemma ignored all the commotion around her, trying to focus on what she needed to do right now. She knew she couldn't change the circumstances, but it was down to her how she reacted to it. Obviously the exit ramp was a no-go just now so she would have to backtrack upstairs and find an alternative form of transport. There was no way she was not getting out of here today.

Even if she had to walk the whole way, she would get home.

She knew that Teri parked out on the street, taking her chances with the parking wardens that plagued the area like locusts; maybe she could cadge a ride somewhere.

Sudden movement caught her eye and she saw that Big Nick and Pencil-Neck were now grappling with each other, staggering about like a pair of drunks on a dance floor. Alex had moved away from the fight and looked her way, obviously unsure what to do.

Seeing her colleagues descending so quickly to the point that they were fighting amongst themselves made Gemma's decision so much easier. She ignored them and popped the boot again. The top priority right now was getting home where she could be safe with her family. She realised that it might not be a quick trip – in fact, it was almost guaranteed not to be – and she had to be prepared for that.

Be prepared. Archie knew it as the Scout motto, but for her and Mark it was more than that. It was a mindset that they had grown into over time, and it had served them well. It meant having a back-up emergency fund for when the car broke down or there was an unexpected bill, it meant gathering information and considering options before making a decision, and it meant planning ahead for as many eventualities as they could think of for whatever situation they were looking at.

Gemma grabbed out the Get Home Bag and put it on the concrete floor beside her. She pulled a couple of items from the boot closer while she tried to calm her racing brain. She folded the picnic blanket up and stuffed it into one of the reusable grocery bags. The blanket was a bright red checked one with a black nylon backing, ideal for picnicking when the grass was damp.

She also folded up the blue light-duty tarp that they used as a boot liner and added that to the bag, then the tow rope and the ugly brown and gold checked blanket from the back seat. It covered a large stain where Archie had spilled a drink years ago, and needed a good vacuum to get rid of the dog hair.

That done, Gemma grabbed the torch and packet of wet-wipes from the glovebox, added them to the bag and looked around her.

Big Nick and Pencil-Neck were still pushing and shoving and most of the others were standing around watching. At least, until Amanda tried to get between them and inadvertently got pushed over by Pencil-Neck. Big Nick went ballistic then and started throwing punches while his opponent backpedalled frantically. They went down on the floor behind a car and all Gemma could hear now was muffled cursing and grunting.

'This is bloody terrible.'

She looked up sharply, realising Alex had come over. He was standing there looking lost, watching her.

'What're you doing?' he said.

'I'm going home,' Gemma said. She put the important items from her handbag into the already-full grocery bag and looked at him. 'What're you going to do?'

He shrugged his skinny shoulders. 'I don't know. Go home, I guess. If I can get there.'

'Where do you live?' Gemma realised she didn't actually know much about him. She'd never had a reason to.

'Manukau – The Gardens. What about you?'

'Way past that. About sixty k's.' Gemma opened the bag and pulled out a pair of clothing items. One was a pair of grey cargo pants, the other a black geothermal T-shirt. As smart as her work outfit of black trousers and blue and white striped shirt with a ruffled front was, they were impractical for the current situation.

Alex was looking at her curiously.

'I need to get changed,' she told him.

He flushed and looked awkward. 'Sorry...ahh...right.' He moved away and Gemma kicked off her sneakers.

Using the car as cover she worked as fast as she could, conscious that she was half-clad only metres away from a bunch of co-workers. Mind you, being seen in her sensible cotton Bendon underwear was probably the least of her concerns right now. She dropped her pants and pulled on the cargo pants, then swapped her shirt for the T. She replaced her work socks with a pair of hiking socks from the bag, and put the work ones in the bag as spares. She re-laced her sneakers then folded her work clothes carefully and put them in the boot of the car.

Closing the boot, she saw Alex coming back, cautiously checking that she was fully clothed. He was like a lost sheep. This time he was carrying a small day pack.

'Do you mind if I come with you?' he asked tentatively. 'I mean, we're both going in the same direction.'

Gemma nodded, knowing it made sense. She didn't know Alex but anticipated that today was going to be a long day, and the company would be good. Safety in numbers.

'Okay,' she said. 'Let's go.'

11

I hurried into the big orange and black Mitre 10 Mega.

The first thing I noticed when I got inside was that the lights were about half strength. The second thing was that people were looking confused, looking around as if waiting for something to happen. I was actually surprised they were at work at all.

I grabbed a trolley and went straight to the camping section, just to the left of the entrance. I knew what I wanted and I wasn't waiting.

There was a group of staff and customers crowded around the Customer Service desk to my left and I ignored them. I could hear the crackle of a radio turned up high and the odd word, but I definitely got the tone.

Urgent and sombre. Typical politicians.

I didn't care what the Prime Minister was going to say so there was no point in standing around to listen. I bet they had their contingencies in place, and fuck the taxpayers.

Taking advantage of the lack of competition right now – I knew for damn sure that it wouldn't last long – I grabbed more butane canisters, a couple of camping stoves and lanterns, cooking sets, candles, torches and batteries. The shelves had definitely been picked over but there was still enough to keep me happy for now. It never ceased to amaze me how slow people were to react to changing circumstances, even in a crisis.

I turned and hurried to the checkout, finding that all the checkout operators were huddled together listening to a radio as well. They didn't even look up at me.

'Excuse me,' I said loudly, and one of the staff glanced round at me. She looked like she'd seen a ghost. 'Can I get some help here?'

She was in shock and just stared at me.

'Now?' I didn't want to be overbearing but I also didn't have time to waste. This was supposed to be just a quick run back into Pukekohe to get the things I hadn't got earlier.

The sales attendant was a young girl, probably a student or even in her first job, and what she had just heard had clearly knocked her for a six.

'The Prime Minister,' she said, gesturing vaguely towards the radio behind her. 'I can't believe it...'

I felt like saying that I couldn't believe she was the Prime Minister either; I never voted for her. Maybe if the Prime Minister had been stronger, maybe if the Government had made better decisions, maybe if the crisis down south had been better managed, maybe we wouldn't be in this position today.

So many maybes and none of them mattered to me right now. Not one single bit. All that mattered was getting my family together and keeping them safe.

And God help anyone that got in my way.

The girl looked at her register screen and frowned. 'It's not working,' she said. She hit some keys and checked the register behind her for the next aisle.

'Probably because the power's low,' I said as patiently as I could. 'I've got cash.'

'I still need to scan the items though,' she said, her tone confused and vague. This was not a scenario they got taught at checkout school.

'Give me a pen and paper,' I said. 'I'll write down what I've got here and tally it up.'

She responded to my commands and while she did so, I became aware that everyone previously huddled over the radios was starting to move. The broadcast was over. People were talking, some hushed and some agitated. A manager of some sort appeared on the scene and tried to herd the staff together.

I took the pen and paper from the girl, who told me she better go and listen to what the manager had to say. I let her go while I scribbled out my shopping list. I had it tallied up by the time she came back. I handed her the list and the pen, followed by a sheaf of cash. It was over by a few dollars but that was okay.

The girl took it and looked at it blankly. 'I don't know what to do with this,' she said.

I ignored the comment. 'Have you got the key for the gas bottles outside?'

'No, Shona does.' She waved at another woman over at the Customer Service desk. 'Shona?'

'Thank you,' I said, checking the girl's name badge, 'Eliza.'

I steered my trolley out the door, seeing Shona behind me. She was an older lady and bustled along like older ladies do. She was shaking her head as she dug out a set of keys.

'Isn't it terrible,' she said, 'just terrible news.'

'You're not wrong there,' I agreed. We stopped beside the large steel wire enclosure that housed the LPG bottles. It was festooned with hazard warning signs.

'Just the one, love?' she asked.

I checked the remaining cash in my pocket. 'How much are they?'

'A few cents under seventy each,' she said.

'I'll take five,' I said. I didn't want to use all my cash up just yet, even though we had a stash back at home.

Her eyes widened.

'I'll just bring the trailer down,' I said, not giving her a chance to protest.

By the time I'd thrown my latest purchases in the back of the truck and pulled up beside the enclosure, Shona had been joined by her manager. Unlike her and Eliza, he was a man who seemed to realise the position we all now found ourselves in.

'Did you want five?' he said.

I nodded.

'Sorry sir, I have to restrict the sales and we can only give you one.' He looked genuinely regretful, but he was also standing firm. 'You've obviously heard the news, so you know the situation.'

'I do,' I agreed. 'And that's exactly why I asked for five.' I held up my notes. 'I've got the cash to pay for it, and when I made the arrangement with your lady here, there was no restriction in place.'

'I understand that sir, but things have changed. Everybody is going to be wanting these, everyone will need to be able to cook and use heating and everything, so I have to be fair and share the sales around.'

He was about my size and strong looking, a bit older than me. His name tag said Dave. I got the impression that arguing with him would solve nothing. I could try and force the issue physically, but he was only trying to be fair. And I wasn't a thug.

I nodded my acceptance of his decision and handed over seventy bucks. I was picking up my 9kg cylinder when two more guys pulled up at the kerb in a hurry. They were rough looking dudes in a shitty grey Mazda sedan.

'Don't lock it, miss,' one called out, rolling out of the passenger door.

I carried my cylinder over to the truck and loaded it into the back. No need to use the trailer now since they were being rationed.

I heard arguing behind me and glanced over. The two guys were fired up, arguing with Dave while Shona stood by helplessly. No doubt they didn't like his restrictions either, but unlike me, they lacked self-control.

I decided to ignore it. I needed to get home and besides, I was no longer a cop. This wasn't my problem. I saw Dave take a sudden step back as he was pushed by one guy while the other grabbed a couple of bottles and moved towards the car. I opened the driver's door of the truck.

'I'll fuckin' smash you, cunt,' one of the guys was yelling, and through the truck windows I saw Dave backpedalling. A few other customers were milling about, but nobody intervened. These were rough dudes and they were intimidating.

One was swinging at Dave now, and the other was tossing LPG cylinders into the back of their car.

Fuck it. Enough was enough.

The aluminium baseball bat was scarred and battered, but strong and it swung well. So well that my first swing took out the assailant's right leg directly behind the knee. He howled and clutched at it, forgetting all about Dave for now. He turned towards me, bellowing something I couldn't understand and hopping on his good leg.

'Get the fuck outta here,' I told him, pointing the bat at him so he knew I meant business.

He yelled again and I heard running feet behind me. I ducked, side stepped, and swung the bat around. The other guy had grabbed a length of wood from the car and was coming at me with it, ready to take my head off. By the time I turned he was almost on me and the timber was arcing through the air at head height. If it had connected it would probably have killed me.

The baseball bat took him across the midsection, hard enough to break his stride. I straightened up, stepped around behind him, and belted him full noise across the side of his right knee. The knee folded in like a puppet with cut strings and he went down screaming, dropping his piece of wood. The other guy was trying to hobble towards me, still mouthing off and dry spit flying from his lips.

Dave was standing off to the side with Shona, his nose bloodied. The customers had all backed away or gone for their cars.

'You two,' I called to them, 'get those cylinders out of their car.'

Dave and Shona moved to do so, and the hobbling guy eyeballed me.

'I know who you are, arsehole,' he panted, 'you're a fuckin' pigshit. Yeah I know you.'

His face seemed vaguely familiar to me, and it took a moment to click. 'I know you too, you're one of the Roimata pieces of shit.'

I couldn't recall his first name, but his family were Black Power from Pukekohe North – the area known as the Reservation, or Rezzo. I'd had dealings with them before.

'You fuckin' know us, cunt,' he said, doing his best to sneer, 'you fuckin' know you fucked up. I'm gonna get you, you fuckin' pigshit cunt.'

'No,' I said evenly, 'what you're gunna do is get in your piece of shit car. Then you're gunna get the fuck outta here before you get a real lesson in manners.' I pointed at his mate who was sitting up and whimpering. 'And take your girlfriend with you.'

Dave and Shona had finished recovering the stolen gas cylinders by now, and I watched as Roimata and his mate dragged themselves to the car. Roimata got in the driver's seat while his mate manoeuvred himself onto the back seat. I moved around the car to keep an eye on Roimata and make sure he didn't pull any other weapons.

'Next time I see you, motherfucker,' he said, 'I'm gonna kill you.'

'There better not be a next time,' I told him. 'I'm not a cop anymore.'

'Got no powers then,' he said.

'Got no limits either.'

He cocked a finger pistol at me and smirked as he fired it. His smile disappeared when I swung the bat again and cracked his window. He pulled back, cursing at me.

'Get moving,' I told him.

He drove off in a cloud of abuse and exhaust fumes, and I stepped back onto the kerb. Dave and Shona looked more shocked than before. I sucked in a breath and felt my pulse start to slow again. My hands were trembling with adrenaline.

'Thank you,' Dave said, his voice quavering. 'I thought they were going to kill me.'

'I thought you were going to kill them,' Shona blurted out.

'Guys like that only understand one thing,' I said. 'They're just bullies. You might want to get some security down here though. This is just the start of it.'

'Oh, I wouldn't think...' Shona started to say, but Dave was nodding.

'I think you're right,' he said. 'We've only just had the announcement. If this is how idiots are acting now, I hate to think how it's going to change.' He dabbed at his nose and gestured towards the enclosure. 'Here, grab a couple of bottles as a thank you.'

'I won't say no.'

It seemed like a reasonable compromise and besides, I hadn't finished here yet. The Roimata's were bad people and I knew it wouldn't take long for the jungle drums to start beating. I could well end up with a posse of fired up gangsters rolling down here to get their revenge.

Thugs like that didn't like being stood up to, and they were very brave in a pack. I didn't like backing down either, but I also had a family to worry about. No point getting my head stoved in, or worse, just to save my ego. Luckily there was no way they could know where I lived.

As I put the cylinders away, I noticed a guy standing at the door of the outdoors supplies shop in the next block of the Supa Centre. He stayed in the shadows of the doorway but I was pretty sure he had a weapon at his side. He saw me looking and stepped back inside.

I sensed Dave approaching as I closed the canopy hatch. His nose had stopped bleeding but he was agitated.

'Thanks again,' he said, putting his hand out. We shook. 'I don't know what those guys would've done if you hadn't been here.'

I nodded. 'They would've taken all your gas bottles and beaten the shit out of you,' I told him honestly. 'Then they would've come back and robbed the store because it was easy the first time. They still might.' I reconsidered that. 'In fact, they probably will.'

He nodded his agreement. 'I think you're right. We're gunna have to do something about that.'

'Don't rely on the cops,' I said, 'they'll be over-stretched already. You'll need to take responsibility for it yourselves, but remember that the law still applies, if that makes sense.'

'Not really. You just beat two guys with a baseball bat. I'd say one of them will probably never walk properly again.'

'He can drag himself by his lips for all I care,' I said, and Dave visibly flinched. 'I responded to their violence with only enough force to overcome them. I couldn't have taken them on safely just hand to hand, and I didn't shoot them.' I shrugged. 'They set the play and they lost.'

Dave nodded again, and I could see that he got it. 'Fair enough. So you're a cop?'

'Was.' I secured the locking handles on the canopy. 'Anyway Dave, I need to grab some timber.'

'I'll meet you down there,' he said. 'If you can give me some advice on securing this place then I'm sure we can work out a good deal.'

I nodded my head towards the outdoors store. 'First place I'd start is over there. They have a bunch of guys working there, bound to be a couple who are happy to scratch your back if you scratch theirs. Plus, if those turkeys come back they're likely to be armed, and that shop's full of guns.'

Dave's mouth turned down. 'I don't know if we can put armed guards at the doors, you know? That might be a bit extreme.'

I shrugged. 'Up to you mate, I don't run the show. You probably couldn't yesterday. But yesterday was a different day; I don't think the same rules apply anymore.'

He frowned.

'Remember the LA riots in '92? After the Rodney King thing?'

Dave nodded quizzically.

'Ever see the footage of the riots where a bunch of Korean shop-keepers guarded their stores? All of them were armed and ready to respond.' I could see the realisation dawning in his face. 'None of them got robbed. There's always an easier target than the place with an armed guard.'

Dave nodded slowly, chewing it over.

'Up to you,' I said. 'But I choose not to be a victim.'

12

B y the time they reached Ngatea the density of traffic had picked up.

The state highway ran through the small town centre, which consisted of half a klick of shops on either side with a river at the east end and open countryside at the west. The Hauraki Plains spread out in all directions, flat and windy even on a day with no wind.

Rob slid into the kerb near a café and cut the engine. The self-serve gas station across the road had a long snake of cars winding into it and the pumps were working, so he guessed the power was still on here. For now, at least.

Sandy popped into the café, their normal stop on the way to Gemma and Mark's. She was back in a few minutes with coffees, sandwiches and a mini quiche each. They joined a flow of traffic heading northwest and ate on the go.

'Okay, what's this?' Rob braked as the cars ahead slowed.

Sitting high in the motorhome he could see over the top of most of the cars. Up ahead were flashing red and blue lights. There were no cars coming the other way.

'Must be a crash,' Sandy mused. She crumpled her sandwich bag and checked her phone again. 'Ooh, I've got a signal.'

It was only one bar but enough to make a connection, and as they sat idling the phone started pinging with incoming messages. A follow up from Mark, suggesting they bring the bus. One from Gemma confirming she had got Mark's message and was on the way. Sandy's brother in Dunedin, checking they were okay. A couple of friends checking in. A reminder from the dentist for Rob's appointment the next day.

'I don't think you'll be going to that, somehow,' Sandy said.

Rob grunted, concentrating on the traffic ahead.

She tapped out a message to Gemma and sent it, and was still typing one to her brother when they finally reached the crash site. There was a single cop in attendance along with a fire crew. A car was in the ditch on the other side and two more were banged up nose to tail and sitting on the shoulder of the road. A man with a bloodied face was being tended to by a firefighter.

Rob noticed that the cop had a pistol holstered on his belt beneath his fluoro vest. He buzzed the window half down as he got alongside the cop and the fire crew chief.

'I can't even get Comms on the radio,' the cop was saying, frustration clear in his tone. 'It's like there's no signal.'

'I've lost the connection again,' Sandy said, frowning at her phone.

'Same with ours,' the fire chief was saying, checking his own portable radio. 'This is not good.'

The cop glanced up at the motorhome and realised Rob was listening. 'Keep moving there mate, you're holding up the traffic.'

Rob nodded and moved ahead, buzzing up his window.

Knowing that the emergency services couldn't contact their own control rooms didn't fill him with confidence.

13

I pulled up outside the camping store shortly afterwards, the trailer now loaded with the stuff I had been after.

Sure enough, one of the staff was standing just inside the doorway and as I crossed the threshold I saw the semi-auto shotgun leaning casually against the wall beside him. He saw me clock it and met my eye firmly. He was a young guy who I had spoken to there before. I had an idea he was the boss' son.

'Alright mate?' he said.

'Yeah, you?'

'Good.' He glanced away, scanning the car park again.

There were several staff in the store, like there always was, and they were all busy. It took me a moment to realise what was going on.

They were shifting the stock around in the floor displays, pushing the cheaper and lesser quality stuff towards the front and moving the better, big ticket items towards the rear. I noticed a second staff member stationed to the other side of the store front, leaning against a wall beside a tall poster that advertised a clothing brand. The bulge behind the poster told me there was a second shotgun ready at hand.

These guys were taking things seriously alright.

A few small groups and individuals were shopping, and by the looks of what they were grabbing they had also accepted the reality of the situation we now faced. Everybody was quiet and focussed, no panicking, just a mind-set of get-in-get-out.

I ignored the fishing and camping stuff and went straight to the counter at the rear. As I got closer the owner/manager emerged from the back office. He was an older guy named Ken, a bloke who totally lived and breathed the outdoors. He looked flushed in the face and greeted me with a grim smile and a crushing hand shake.

'Alright mate?'

Maybe the boy at the front was his son, after all.

Racks of rifles and shotguns lined the wall behind him, and the glass display cabinets held air pistols, knives, and accessories. There was a room off behind the counter with more firearms on display.

'All good mate.' I tossed my chin at the busy workers. 'Good idea. Had any trouble yet?'

'Some hoods from the Rezzo came in demanding this that and the other. The boys sorted them out pretty quick, but not before they'd nicked a few bits and pieces and broke a display. Fuckin' arseholes.' He sat down heavily on a stool behind the counter, clearly happy to take a break.

'I see you're a bit better prepared now.'

He looked at me sharply. 'Not a problem, is it? I'm not gunna let those pricks just roll in and help themselves.'

'It's a good idea mate. I'd do the same.' I thought about the Browning I had stashed under my car seat and the Rossi under a blanket in the foot well. I didn't want to be away from the truck for too long.

'Had a couple of yobbos too, when he news first come out. Just country boys. Came in wanting guns and ammo to hold off the Indonesian invasion.' He gave a wry smile. 'I told them it wasn't fuckin' *Red Dawn* and they'd be welcome to come back with their licenses or somebody I knew. Didn't like that too much.' He grunted. 'Too fuckin' bad. I still got a business to run, and I got my own family to worry about too.' He waved a hand towards his workers. 'That includes my boys and girls here.'

'Fair enough too.' I dug out my firearms licence and put it on the counter. 'I need a few things myself.'

'Oh yeah.' He heaved himself off his stool. 'The usual?'

'Yeah, I need .22 long, .357 Magnum, and twelve gauge – double ought and number four.'

'Uh-huh.' He wiped the back of his gnarled hand across his mouth. 'How much?'

'A thousand of each. Plus half that of nine mil.' I thought for a second. 'Got any three-oh-three?'

'Not a lot, how much d'you want?'

'Five hundred?' A thought occurred to me. 'Long shot, but I don't s'pose you've got any chargers for a Lee Enfield have you?'

He wasn't fazed. 'No worries. And of course I've got chargers – what kinda gun shop would this be if I didn't? Those old bang-sticks are still popular, y'know son.' He glanced around then leaned in closer and looked me in the eye. 'I'm tryin' not to worry these guys, but it's obvious this is bigger than they're saying. I know you'll know. What's the word?'

I felt a kick in the back of my brain, that kick you get when your conscience is telling you to do the right thing. Old Ken was a good man and he was trying to do the right thing; all he wanted was information. But what was the consequence of giving up what I knew? How far would he spread it? One, two, ten people? They spread it to another hundred, a thousand, and panic grows and spreads faster than wildfire.

Or hold it back and have Ken know I held out on him?

'I don't know more than anyone else, mate,' I told him softly. 'I'm outta the loop now. But you're no slug, and it seems to me that you're doing all the right things. You're in a good position here to look after yourselves and your families, so I'd carry on doing what you're doing.'

Ken nodded slowly, his eyes still on mine. I got the feeling he knew I was still holding back some, but I hadn't fobbed him off either.

'I need to get going,' I said. 'The only other thing I can really say is that I don't think the worst has come yet. Keep an ear on the news.'

Ken wiped his face again, pausing only to grab one of his staff as she went past and give her a scribbled note he'd made. 'Right,' he said finally, 'you better come round and give me a hand.'

I wasted no time in getting around the counter and stacking boxes by the till. These guys weren't the cheapest in town but they were reasonable, and they never tried to flog off smoky Chinese shit ammo. And he was right; he did have half a dozen chargers for the Lee Enfield. They were obviously old but still looked serviceable, and I trusted that Ken wouldn't try to flog them off if they weren't.

He got side-tracked with another customer who was negotiating on a rifle with one of the staff, while I filled my mental shopping list. When he came back he glanced at the stacked ammo.

'That's a fair whack there, mate.'

'You're not wrong, mate.' I had cash but wasn't sure if it would cover the lot. I pulled the wad from my pocket, and Ken looked at it.

'I just heard you sorted out some arseholes over the way there,' he said.

I continued counting. 'Unfortunately someone had to.' I was nearly at the end of my cash and we could both see I was short. Well short.

Ken glanced at the money in my hand then looked me in the eye. He gave me a short nod.

'Take it,' he said. 'Just take it and get goin'.'

I didn't argue. 'Thanks Ken, I appreciate it.'

Since he was in a giving mood I added a couple more bricks to the pile. While I took the first armful out to the truck, he started unlocking a security bar on one of the displays. When I came back inside from the next load, Ken had laid a semi-auto shotgun on the counter.

'You still got that lever action Rossi I sold you?' he said. 'And the Mossberg?'

'Yep.'

'You don't have anything better suited for, ahh...more selective fire?'

'Nope. You know me Ken, I'm Mr Low-tech.'

He grunted. 'Shame,' he said. 'I'd let you have this but it's my last one. You'll have to rely on what you've got.' He gave me a crooked smile. 'I'm pretty sure you'll be okay. Wait here a sec.'

Ken disappeared to his back office and returned in a moment with a cardboard box in one hand. I could see it was a case of Back Country freeze dried meals. They weren't cheap but they were nutritious and light to carry. I hesitated, unsure whether to accept the gift or not – as much as I wanted it. Ken twigged and waved his hand dismissively.

'Don't worry about me, mate.' He gestured at the walls around him. 'I got a whole shop full of stuff; I'll be okay. And if it's a false alarm I trust you to return everything to me, right?'

'Fair enough.' I nodded. 'Make sure you keep a note. I threw in another couple more bricks of .22 and double-ought.'

'I saw that. It's all good. I know you're good for it.'

I didn't know what to say. When the chips are down the best people really do come to the fore, and in a bizarre kind of way, it seems to make some people more generous than normal.

'Now get goin'.'

My heart was racing and I felt a lump in my throat. 'Thank you,' I said. I stuck out my hand and we shook. 'You take care of yourself.'

'You too.' Ken turned away and started loading shells into the shotgun.

I turned and left without a word. It was time to get home and get some of my own preparations underway.

14

The fighting had somehow ended but everyone still seemed to be standing around. There was a lot of agitated talking and hand gestures but no real action.

Gemma didn't wait around. She headed to the stairs with Alex in tow and her Get Home Bag over her shoulder. They had both moved their cars back to their parking spots and left them locked. She could hear other people in the stairwell above them, loud talking in panicked voices.

They passed a group of three who were heading for the car park and Gemma paused to tell them that the exit was blocked.

'Are you sure?' one of the guys asked, frowning at her. He was a young guy with curly hair and glasses. She thought he was maybe from Customer Services.

'Yes, I'm sure,' she replied tersely, 'it happened right in front of us.'

She made to carry on up the stairs but he stopped her with a hand on her arm. 'You can't be right,' he said, a condescending tone to his voice. 'That just doesn't sound right.'

'It is,' she said, shooting him a look.

She shook her arm free and he gave her a look of annoyance. 'Jeez, keep your hair on, sweetie.'

'Sweetie?' Gemma gave him a cold look. 'Seriously? I'm probably old enough to be your mother.'

He opened his mouth to retort but one of the others ushered him along and they carried on down the stairs. Gemma could hear him continuing to mouth off as they hit the next flight down, but she ignored him and continued upwards. They reached the ground floor and emerged into Reception.

Teri was crossing the floor towards the front doors, her jacket on and her bag over her shoulder.

She stopped by the door when she saw them coming. 'Where have you been? Have you heard what's going on?'

'Yeah we heard. We're heading home but some jerk blocked the exit ramp and we can't get our cars out.'

'Jesus.' Teri's face was pale. She was a decade younger than Gemma, a nice girl who lived with her boyfriend. Their wedding was only a few months away and she was desperately trying to lose weight for it. 'It's pretty scary eh?'

'It's serious,' Gemma agreed. 'Are you going home?'

Teri pushed the door open to the entrance foyer. There were lifts and more doors to the stairs over to the left and the main front doors to the building to the right, the centre of the glass-fronted building. Other people from the other businesses in the building were bustling about and the exit doors were held open by a constant stream of people going to and fro.

'I think everyone is,' Teri said. 'Melinda just told me to shut up shop and get going.'

Gemma nodded, hearing a faint rumble as they started to cross the atrium-like foyer. She cocked her head, noticing other people doing likewise. She saw the people closest to the door staring out into the street and she followed their gaze.

'Oh my God,' Teri said, pointing.

The rumble continued, getting louder, and Gemma heard a new sound now. A popping followed a clatter. It took her a moment to spot the origin of the noise.

Out in the street she could see smoke and some kind of objects sailing through the air.

'What the hell?' Alex said in amazement.

A woman screamed and people started to back away from the doors.

Manhole covers in the road were exploding upwards, hurtling into the sky under the pressure of the flames bursting up from beneath them. As each hole on the road was exposed more smoke and flames burst forth, columns of flame shooting upwards like geysers. Each eruption was accompanied by a cloud of dust and debris, the clouds rolling down the street into each other.

Everybody stopped and stared, transfixed by the bizarre spectacle as it got closer. The rumble was getting rapidly louder and the floor was trembling beneath their feet.

A manhole cover out at the kerb closest to them shot into the sky in a cloud of smoke and angry orange flame.

'Gas lines,' Alex said. 'Oh shit!'

He turned, grabbing Gemma and Teri and pushing them away as the glass front wall exploded inwards.

They tumbled to the floor in a tangle of arms and legs, sliding on the polished tiles as a pressure wave rolled over them and shattered glass fragments went everywhere, showering them like confetti.

Gemma got her arms over her head and scrunched her eyes shut tight, feeling her body being buffeted by unseen forces, the weight of somebody across her shoulders holding her down. Her ears were ringing and there was an alarm screeching somewhere.

A stillness descended and she forced her eyes open. Glass was everywhere and people were screaming. The air felt hot and she could smell gas. Alex moved off her and she climbed to her feet, helping Teri up. The three of them looked at each other and Gemma wondered if she looked as shocked as the other two.

'What the bloody hell was that?' Teri quavered.

'Gas pipes underground,' Alex said with some certainty. 'They're blowing.'

'No shit.'

The entire front of the ground floor was blown inwards and Gemma could see a car on fire out at the kerb. As she looked further she could see more damage. At least half a dozen cars on fire, actually. Trees overhanging a boundary fence across the road were aflame and a ruptured water main had also burst, jetting skywards.

Car alarms were going outside and in the building there was another siren shrieking. The water sprinklers hadn't activated, so Gemma presumed it was an intruder or panic alarm rather than a fire alarm.

She realised someone was screaming as well and spotted a huddle of people near where the front doors used to be. They were from one of the other businesses' upstairs. A woman was slumped against the wall with a hand clamped to her face, blood flowing between her fingers. Another woman standing beside her was screaming for the Olympics and a man kneeling beside the injured woman was shouting at the screamer to shut up and call an ambulance.

Gemma felt a jab in her neck and brushed a piece of glass from her collar. She put her bag down and shook herself, brushing more fragments from her hair and clothing.

'Oh my bloody God,' Alex whispered.

Gemma followed his gaze and recoiled in horror. A man she didn't recognise was leaning against the wall several metres away, hunched over and holding both hands to the front of his white business shirt. He was well dressed, maybe early thirties.

The shirt was bright red and a stream of red was running down his pants to the floor, puddling round his shiny shoes.

Gemma froze, watching as the man slid down the wall ever so slowly. His butt hit the floor and his legs sprawled out in front of him. His face was as white as the collar of his shirt.

'Jesus!'

She felt herself moving forward, her legs on auto-pilot, knowing they had to help him. The size of the blood puddle around the guy wasn't promising. She'd never been good with blood or emergency-type situations; that was Mark's domain. She was better at providing comfort afterwards, but something told her that this man wouldn't be needing that.

'Watch out!'

Gemma heard the shouted warning and looked round in confusion, unsure what it was about.

She didn't have time to see who had shouted, the cracking of timber above her head drawing her attention instead. Looking up, she saw the glass ceiling of the atrium was caving in. The wooden framing was broken and great sheets of glass were falling through the air.

Her feet slipped on the debris beneath her as she scrabbled to get away, throwing herself towards the furthest away wall where a great steel pillar rose up like a beacon of safety. She hit the floor and slid on her front, glass fragments stabbing at her, her hands outstretched like she was diving for the corner flag.

There was a deafening crash as the ceiling hit the floor and exploded into a billion pieces. Gemma's hands slammed into the wall, followed painfully by her shoulder and hip. She covered her head and cowered against the wall, trying to curl herself into the pillar for what little protection it could offer her.

Screams and cries were echoing around the atrium and Gemma raised her head. She could feel the prickle of broken glass everywhere she made contact with the floor, and she quickly scrambled to her feet. Alex and Teri were picking themselves up as well, shaking glass from their clothes and hair. Both of them had eyes like saucers.

The injured man against the wall opposite her was no longer moving, his hands lying slack at his side. He was lolling like a drunk but he was clearly way past that.

Gemma averted her eyes, knowing he was dead and not wanting to see it. The huddle of people by the front doors were still there, but the screaming woman was crouching now, whimpering like a child.

The man who had been yelling at her to shut up had forgotten all about her and the woman with the bleeding face. Instead, he was trying to staunch the flow of blood from a large gash to his thigh. As Gemma stared, she could see blood squirting from between his fingers every time he moved. Not just squirting, but actually jetting out like a hose released under pressure.

She knew that wasn't good. The guy shifted his hand slightly and a jet of red burst forth, arcing a good few metres across the floor. Gemma started to move towards him to help, but froze when she heard a distinct creaking sound from above.

She didn't wait around to look. 'Run!'

She sprinted for the exit, her feet sliding on the broken glass as she tried to get traction. People were moving, panicking, crashing into each other without care. Someone went down and got trampled underfoot. Gemma could sense runners all around her but ignored them, focussing instead on keeping one foot in front of the other and getting the hell out of there.

She crossed the threshold and was almost to the front steps when there was a thunderous crash behind her in the atrium as the roof came down completely. Someone collided with her from behind and she felt herself thrown forward, smacking into someone else and going down in a tangle of bodies. She landed on top of someone, hearing grunts and shouts all around her, rolling and tumbling until she hit the concrete at the base of the steps and came to a stop beside the footpath.

The air was filled with dust and smoke and the stench of gas and burning cars was strong.

Gemma lay still for a few moments, gathering herself before gingerly getting to her feet. She was sore and shaken but couldn't detect any injuries. Others were rising around her, some looking confused, some looking distressed. Everyone was dusty and dishevelled.

Some were bloodied and she saw one guy cradling a dislocated shoulder and moaning.

She spotted Alex nearby and joined him, waiting while he dusted himself off.

'You okay?' she asked.

He nodded and rubbed a hand over his face. It was grimy and pale. 'I think so.'

Gemma cocked her head to the side. 'I can hear sirens.'

'I don't see any cops or fire engines,' he said, scanning around them. 'Has someone called an ambulance?'

Gemma didn't answer, looking instead for Teri. She saw her further down the footpath, huddled together with Melinda, the older lady she worked with at Reception. Melinda was in tears and it looked like Teri was trying to console her. There were other huddles forming, as if they were all standing around for a fire drill, waiting for the all-clear from the people in yellow hi-viz vests.

Teri spotted Gemma and Alex and brought Melinda over to them. Gemma patted Melinda's back sympathetically.

'It's awful,' the older woman said, wiping at her eyes, 'just awful.'

'Did you see that guy?' Teri asked in hushed tones. 'Inside?'

The mention of it set Melinda off again and Alex put an arm around her shoulders. 'I don't think anyone could have helped him,' he said awkwardly, obviously unsure how to deal with her. He looked to Gemma, silently pleading for help.

Gemma gave him an apologetic shrug and got her cell phone out, hoping for a signal. No service. She put it away again and turned to Teri.

'What're your plans, Teri?' she asked. 'Are you going home?'

Her friend looked confused. 'Yeah, I guess so. I mean, we're allowed to, right?'

Gemma looked around them. Huddles of people, everyone in shock, a few trying to get through or over the piled debris in the smashed entrance to the building. A guy she didn't recognise was climbing over the rubble, looking over his shoulder and shouting to those near him, trying to rally some assistance.

It was Gemma's natural instinct to help, but two things were holding her back: the fear that the building would collapse even further, and the tug inside to get home. Looking up at the office building, she could see serious cracks in the facing. Windows on higher levels were cracked as well and she knew it wouldn't take long before they started to come down. She stepped back involuntarily.

'I think we need to move,' she said, glancing over to Alex and Teri.

'Where's your car, Teri? Can you give us a lift, at least part of the way?'

Teri pointed down the road towards the residential area where she always parked. It was very limited parking there but she always seemed to get a spot.

'Right,' Gemma said, injecting some strength into her voice. It was not time to dilly-dally about now. 'Melinda, what're you going to do?'

Melinda had gathered herself together to some degree, or had at least stopped crying. 'I think I'll go home. I've got to find Lisa though, she drove today.'

Gemma knew the older woman always carpooled with a colleague who lived in her suburb. She spotted Lisa in another group of people further down the footpath, and pointed her out.

'There she is,' she said, 'away you go. Good luck.'

She shooed Melinda away and turned to her two colleagues. 'Right,' she said, 'let's go.'

They dutifully fell in behind her as she hurried off down the footpath, ignoring everyone else around them. There were more office buildings in that part of the street and they skirted round the occupants who had emerged, heading for Teri's blue Suzuki hatchback. The manhole covers had stopped exploding but the fires still burned.

Gemma noticed smoke coming from a residential property further along and presumed it had been hit by the gas fires. What were the chances that the gas lines would explode? She didn't know. If they blew, would they wipe out the block? Again, she didn't know. One thing she did know was that she didn't feel safe where they were.

Teri bleeped the locks and Gemma took the passenger seat. She knew that Teri lived near Cornwall Park, so getting a ride that far would save a big walk. With any luck they may be able to organise another ride or borrow a car to take them the rest of the way. She could drop Alex off on the way past Manukau and carry on home.

She buckled up as Teri started the car. Alex was settling himself in the backseat. Smoke was drifting across the street and she could see a few other cars starting to move off as well. She turned and looked at Teri. They both took a breath.

'Let's go,' Gemma said.

15

We normally had the radio going and the house was quiet without it, the sort of quiet you could never get in the city. Birds chirped outside, the grass rustled in the wind and a cow mooed somewhere in a neighbouring paddock.

Archie was playing outside with Jethro and my mother was in the spare room that she was using, probably trying to get hold of my brother.

I set about getting food organised for dinner in the first instance, chopping vegetables and slicing the blade steak from the freezer. We were supposed to be having a beef casserole in the crockpot, but the day we were having was far from the day we had planned. A stir-fry on the barbeque was the new plan. As long as it had noodles, Archie would eat it.

I wondered how long our power would last. The solar panels on the roof were linked up to the grid but we didn't have our own batteries for storage, so I wasn't holding my breath.

I watched from the kitchen window as Archie threw a ball on the front lawn for Jethro. He didn't like getting dog slobber on his hands so after a few throws he changed to a stick. Jethro didn't care; he'd play fetch all day long with his buddy.

I scraped the meat off the plastic chopping board into a bowl and washed the board. I made up a simple sauce with soy and honey and crushed two cloves of garlic into it. I was nearly finished when I heard my mother behind me.

'How're you doing, sunshine?' she said. She came and leaned against the bench beside me.

I put the garlic crusher in the sink and wiped my hands. 'Fine. Worried about Gemma, worried about what's going to happen.' I shrugged. 'I dunno, it's all a waiting game isn't it?'

She nodded. 'Sure is, kiddo.'

Archie laughed as Jethro overshot the stick and tumbled as he tried to grab it. His laughter always brought a smile to my face, even today.

'Whatever happens,' I said, 'and however long this situation lasts,' I jerked a thumb in his direction, 'that needs to never be lost.'

She nodded again, her eyes on me. 'That's right.'

'And we as a family,' I continued, 'need to remain safe.' I held her gaze for a moment. 'And tight.'

She gave me that look she'd always given me when she was getting defensive; chin up, a challenging look in her eye.

'Oh yes,' she said, 'you don't need to tell me that, kiddo.'

Again with the kiddo. Letting me know who was boss. I took a short breath.

'I know that Gemma and her parents aren't high on your Christmas card list, Mum,' I said. 'So I do think that needs to be said. We're gunna have enough on our plate without battling each other.'

'What d'you mean, battling each other?' She was well on the defensive now. 'I've never had a problem with any of them. We get on fine. Why, have they said something?'

'Nobody's said anything, Mum, and don't make this into a big deal. But we're all going to be here together for who knows how long, so we need to get along. There's no room for little digs or one-upman-ship, is there?'

Her jaw was set and her eyes were hot. 'And I take it everyone's going to be getting this little speech, are they Mark? Or is it just me being singled out?'

I took another breath. This was never going to be an easy conversation, but I was wishing I could rewind two minutes. Or maybe twenty years.

'Anyone that needs it, will get the same message,' I said evenly. 'So please just take it in the spirit that I'm giving it.'

'Well I don't appreciate being spoken to like that,' she snapped back, 'and I certainly don't appreciate being singled out as if I'm the one with a problem.'

I'd had enough and that little switch, the safety catch inside my brain that kept me in check, clicked off.

'Look,' I said, 'I've got more things to worry about right now than your ego. I'm asking you to keep your tongue in check and pitch in. This is not going to be easy for any of us, and I don't need you stirring up shit with the other people in my family. If you can't do that then we've got a big problem, Mum. And I can do without another big problem.'

I could feel my heart pounding hard against my ribs.

'My job is to protect my family, and that's what I'll do. But I don't need knives in my back while I'm doing it.'

We glared at each other for an eternity, before she turned abruptly and walked off. I heard the bedroom door bang shut. I put my hands on my hips and sucked down air, trying to get myself back under control. No such conversation had ever gone well with my mother.

I heard a shuffle behind me and turned to see Archie watching me from the doorway. He had a stick in his hand and his face was a picture of sadness.

'That wasn't very nice, Dad,' he said. 'You shouldn't talk to Grandma like that.'

I rubbed a hand over my face. My hand smelled of garlic.

'Sorry you heard that, buddy. That wasn't a very nice conversation.'

I held out my hands and he came for a cuddle. I lifted him up and held him.

'Sometimes grown-ups don't agree with each other, and we get a bit angry. Just like you do with your buddies at school, eh?'

He nodded into my shoulder and hugged his arms around my neck a bit tighter. I squeezed his little body against me and held him until he pulled away and looked at me.

'Dad? Is Mum coming home soon?'

I gave total confidence my best shot.

'Of course little man, she's on the way home. She might take a while to get here though, so we have to be patient, okay?'

He nodded. 'I miss her. I wish she was here.' The sadness in his eyes punched me straight in the heart. 'I'm worried about her.'

I felt myself welling up at the pure innocence and goodness that only a child can show.

'Don't cry, Dad.'

He wiped my eyes with his little hands just as I did to him when he was upset and I laughed and hugged him tight again.

'I love you, wee man.'

'Love you too, Dad. And you, Grandma.'

I turned and found my mother watching from the doorway. Something had changed in her demeanour, perhaps the slightest of softening, not that she would ever admit it. She gave Archie a twinkly smile.

'I love you too, little man.'

She kissed his cheek over my shoulder and he reached out for her. I let him go, pleased despite everything that he wanted to go to her. She cuddled him and looked at me. I gave a short nod, but I could tell from the determination of her gaze, the hardness lurking back there, that the dust had not settled.

I sighed inwardly. Fuck it, there was only so much I could do.

16

S tate Highway 2 was a long asphalt ribbon that ran all the way from the Bay of Plenty to the Bombay hills at the Auckland-Waikato border.

It was a high crash area and on Sunday evenings and long week-ends it became a parking lot of frustrated holidaymakers. Fortunately traffic seemed normal so far, and Rob felt his tension easing back a notch as they cruised along. The drama at the Paeroa gas station had sent his blood pressure soaring, and he knew that Sandy was feeling it too. He gave her a glance.

'Alright there, my girl?'

She nodded and smiled weakly, not wanting to look him in the eye lest he see her tears.

'We'll be there soon enough,' he assured her. 'Little Archie will probably be home; he'll be glad to see us.'

'I suppose she'll still be there, too,' Sandy said with more than a hint of distaste.

'I guess so.'

'How long's it been?'

Rob chuckled. 'Too long, according to Gem. A week, I think. Her kitchen should be done any day now.'

'She should've gone and stayed with her other son while she got her renovations done,' Sandy said. 'He's her favourite, anyway.'

'True, but Mark's closer,' Rob said.

She pursed her lips and frowned, but said nothing. Rob was well aware of his wife's feelings about Jenny.

'Just smile and do what you do,' he said.

'Of course I will,' she frowned. '*I* won't make it hard.'

He nodded to himself, keeping an eye on the traffic around them. They'd already had one idiot blast past them at a rate of knots, and he had no desire to crash before they even got to Gemma and Mark's.

After a few minutes, Sandy asked, 'How long d'you think we'll need to be there?'

Rob shrugged. 'Don't know. Depends how long this emergency lasts, I guess. Could be a few days. Could be a few weeks.'

Sandy frowned again. 'A few weeks, you reckon? We'll be able to go back home though, won't we?'

Rob sucked his teeth. 'I don't know about that. You saw those clowns back at the gas station. What if that became the norm?'

She looked at him doubtfully and he shrugged again.

'Remember the earthquakes in Christchurch? They had looting going on down there, God knows what else. Hurricane Katrina in the States? Apparently that was like a damn war zone.'

'Yeah, but we're not the States.'

'No we're not,' he agreed. 'We don't have their gun crime and all the crap that goes with that, but we also don't have a massive resource of law enforcement and military like they do.' He jerked a thumb back over his shoulder. 'What we saw back there could just be the start of it.'

'Stop,' Sandy said, 'that's horrible.'

Rob glanced at her again. 'I know it's crappy, my girl, but we need to be prepared for it. This could be a long haul.'

Sandy dug out her phone. 'I'll try them again.'

The tyres hummed on the asphalt as they headed towards the unknown.

17

The roads were already busier than normal and Gemma guessed a lot of others were doing exactly what she, Alex and Teri were – getting the hell out of town.

The traffic was moving, at least so far. She wondered what it would be like in another hour or two, or even another ten minutes. She wondered what was happening back at work and about the people who had been injured and killed. About their families; families that would never get their loved ones home today. Maybe ever. Who knew how long a state of emergency would last?

She wondered what Mark was doing, how Archie was reacting to the situation (probably fine), how Mark's mother Jenny was handling it (probably not fine). She wondered how long it would take her to get home today.

She heard talking and snapped back into the present, realising Teri was speaking to her.

'Sorry,' she said. 'What was that?'

'I was saying I don't know how far we'll be able to go,' Teri said. 'The radio news is just saying that the motorway's jammed already and they're asking people to stay off the roads if they can avoid it.'

'Well we can't avoid it,' Gemma said, feeling her tension ratchet up a good notch. 'We need to get home. One Tree Hill's not far, anyway.' She glanced at her friend. 'We should be alright to get to your place, eh?'

Teri's eyes were fixed on the road and the cars around her. Her knuckles were white on the wheel.

'I don't know, Gem. We'll just keep going and see what happens.'

'If you don't go on the motorway it should be easier,' Alex chimed in from the back seat.

Teri flicked her eyes to the rear view mirror and gave him a look. 'Thanks,' she said. 'I hadn't thought of that.'

'Jeez,' he grumbled, sitting back. 'No need to bite my head off. I was only trying to help.'

She glared at him in the mirror. 'Well it's not a normal fucking day is it, Alex? I don't know what the average day is like in IT, but at Reception we don't normally have buildings blowing up and people dying. And aside from that, my car will probably overheat unless this fucking traffic hurries up, and that'll piss me off too.'

Gemma kept her thoughts to herself and her eyes on the road. Teri didn't normally swear like that, and she had a fair point. The tension in the car was palpable and she didn't want to add to it with pointless chatter. She tuned an ear to the radio instead, but amongst the traffic updates and repeats of the Prime Minister's announcement, there was nothing new.

She ran through a mental checklist of what she had with her. Enough food and water for 24 hours. A torch, basic first aid kit, emergency shelter. Spare pair of socks, a thermal top, a waterproof jacket. Nothing luxurious, but it was enough to get her home if the car broke down or there was some kind of emergency that required her to abandon the car.

A normal emergency, that was. She was pretty sure that Mark hadn't counted on a national state of emergency being declared. He used to joke about the North Koreans and Chinese invading but it had never seriously been something he'd planned for.

She didn't fancy walking all the way home. It was a hell of a hike and would take her probably three days if she was walking in a straight line. She didn't have the supplies for that, and presumably it would mean sleeping rough and taking her chances on the street.

She shuddered at the thought. With any luck she'd be able to get her hands on a car, or even a bike. Maybe the trains would be running and she could get to Pukekohe. Mark and Archie could come and pick her up and she'd be home in no time.

The thought of it lifted her spirits.

They had reached Ponsonby and were tracking south, but it was still slow going. Gemma checked her watch, realising it had been more than forty minutes since they'd left work. The time had slipped by while she was lost in her thoughts, and she wondered what else she had missed.

The radio was still on and she turned the volume up. The announcer was partway through a message.

'...phones are down, I'm guessing they're jammed up with emergency calls, but we have had reports of gas explosions in downtown Auckland and casualties coming in. We don't know the extent of the problems there, or anywhere else around the country to be honest, so all we can do is just hope and pray that people are safe and keeping off the streets.'

'Not by the looks of it,' Alex said.

'There hasn't been any further updates issued from the Prime Minister, at least none that have been received by us, but as soon as we do hear anything we'll be sure to let you know. As we've already said earlier, the latest we've got is that a state of emergency has been declared nationwide...'

Gemma turned the volume back down again. Negativity on a loop would do none of them any good.

'What're your plans when you get home?' she asked Teri.

Her friend barely moved her eyes from the cars in front of her.

'I think I'm gunna sit on my couch and eat chips,' she said. 'Hopefully Andrew will be home.' She risked a glance at Gemma. 'We can eat chips together.'

Gemma raised an eyebrow. 'Really? That's your solution? Sit on the couch and eat chips?'

Teri gave an exaggerated nod. 'Yup. What else can I do?'

Gemma could think of a hundred things better than that plan, and she was debating which one to suggest when she realised her friend was smiling.

'So gullible,' Teri grinned.

Gemma felt a reluctant smile cross her lips. 'Dickhead,' she said.

'Meat and veg,' Teri retorted.

They drove in silence for a while, each of them lost in their own thoughts. They were nearly at Mt Eden when Teri groaned.

Gemma looked up sharply and saw steam rising from beneath the bonnet. 'Uh-oh.'

'Fuckity-fuckity-fuck-fuck!' Teri slapped the steering wheel and groaned again. 'It's all this bloody idling, it always overheats when I'm stuck in traffic for too long.'

'Better pull over,' Alex said.

'Thanks, genius. I hadn't thought of that either.'

She steered to the side of the road and switched it off. 'No point calling the AA, I suppose.'

Gemma checked her phone. 'Still no service anyway.'

'It's alright,' Teri said. 'I've got water, I'll just wait for it to cool down and top it up. It's not far to go now anyway.'

'How far?' Alex said, leaning forward between the seats.

'I don't know, not far.'

'Like, how long to drive in normal traffic?'

'I don't know.' She screwed her nose up at him. 'I don't pay any attention to that, and besides, I normally go on the motorway.'

Gemma checked her watch again. 2.15pm. It was over two hours since Mark had contacted her, a bit less since the official announcement had been made. A lot had happened since then but it felt like she had barely progressed at all.

Her experience with overheating cars told her they would be waiting the better part of an hour before they could get going again, pushing them out past three o'clock. She didn't want to be waiting that long. The traffic was hardly moving, so she didn't fancy their chances of getting very far in the car anyway.

'We need to make a decision,' she said. She turned in her seat so she could see both of them. 'Do we wait here with the car or do we just walk it?'

The other two exchanged looks, neither wanting to take the lead and voice an opinion. Gemma didn't have time to waste.

'I vote we walk,' she said. 'Mt Eden's not far from One Tree Hill, maybe three or four k's? We could easily make that in less than hour.'

'I think it's further than that,' Teri said doubtfully. 'And what about my car?'

'Leave it here. It's not going anywhere anyway.'

'That's still a fair walk,' she said.

Gemma bit back her impatience. 'It's not far. We don't have to set a record, we're not in a race.'

Her friend still looked dubious and Gemma turned to Alex.

'What d'you reckon, Alex? Wait or walk? If Teri's not coming then I'm going to head to the train station and see if they're still running.'

He hefted his bag. 'I'm on for a walk. We can't wait here all day, and I can get a train to Manukau or Manurewa and go from there.'

'Teri?'

Teri chewed her lip silently for a long moment, then shook her head. 'No,' she said. 'I'll stay with the car. It'll be fine.'

Gemma sat for a moment, waiting to see if either of them was going to suggest an alternative plan or if Teri would change her mind. When nothing happened, she cracked her door.

Teri joined them on the footpath and gave them each a big hug. They sorted out rough directions to the Mt Eden train station and checked their gear. Gemma secured the day pack on her back and carried the jute shopping bag with the extra gear. Alex had his own bag on his back. He held out his hand for the shopping bag, but Gemma declined with a smile.

'It's okay, I'll carry it,' she said. She knew it was extra weight and he was only being polite, but she wanted to keep her gear with her.

She had the feeling that today, more than ever before, she needed to rely on herself.

18

R ob spotted the pall of smoke before they hit the tailback, and knew right away that they were in for a wait.

The tailback was at least a couple of k's long already and not moving.

'Is that a fire?' Sandy said, craning to try and get a better angle.

'I'd say a car fire from that black smoke,' Rob said, slipping the bus into neutral. 'The engine's on fire.'

Sandy sighed and sat back. 'I've text them again,' she said. 'I don't know if they're going through though.'

'Have you heard from Carla at all?'

'Not yet...oh, hang on, here we go. Must be in a good spot here.' Her phone pinged as messages came up. 'Carla... "got the messages and will contact you tomorrow. The kids have practice today and Ryan is not home until late so no rush".'

She looked to her husband and he looked at her. It was typical of their oldest daughter.

'I think she's failing to grasp the seriousness of the situation,' Rob grumbled. 'Tell her to get her backside in gear.'

Sandy snorted. 'And when did that ever work? She's got your genes – stubborn as a damn mule.'

Rob let it slide, mostly because he knew it was true. It didn't make him any less worried about his daughter or granddaughters.

'Have you text Ryan as well?' he said, already knowing the answer.

Sandy gave him another look. 'Have you?'

He gave a slight smile. 'I've been busy driving, my girl,' he said.

Sandy frowned and said nothing. She tapped out another quick message to Carla.

We r on the way to GnMs. This is serious.

She was about to hit Send then reconsidered. She added *Luv Mum xxx* and hit Send. She didn't normally add endearments like that, but hopefully it gave the message some emphasis. She put her phone away and looked out the window. It didn't look like they had moved an inch.

'We haven't,' Rob said, as if reading her mind. 'And nothing's coming the other way, either.'

He switched off the engine and they sat. Waiting.

19

The dog raced off after a rabbit and Archie and I watched him go as we crossed the paddock.

The three heifers at the other end chewed grass and watched us. One of them lifted its tail and took a dump before stepping forward a pace and eating some more. Life was simple when you're a heifer. I checked the fence and tracked down the line to the next paddock. Archie walked beside me, swishing a stick through the grass. We were quiet, there being no need to talk just now.

Jethro bounded back to us after a fruitless hunt, a big grin on his face. I was convinced he had missed the "How to catch a Rabbit" tutorial at dog school. He bunted Archie's stick and backed off, shifting his gaze from Archie to the stick in his hand.

'No Jethro,' the boy told him firmly, 'you're not having it. This is my walking stick.'

Jethro wagged his tail and a second later the stick was flying through the air with the dog dashing after it.

'Crazy dog,' Archie said.

I ruffled his hair and was about to speak when I felt the hairs on my neck prickle. I removed my hand from his head and shifted it closer to the Browning I had tucked in my waistband. I couldn't see or hear anything but my sixth sense was pinging.

We reached the end of the paddock and Jethro raced back with the stick in his mouth, dropping it at Archie's feet. I intended to cross into the second paddock and check the fence there too, but I couldn't ignore the feeling that we were being watched.

I paused at the fence we were about to cross, listening hard, and finally clocked a slight movement on the other side of the treeline. I put myself between the trees and Archie.

'Who's there?'

There was a rustle of movement and I saw a figure through a gap in the trees.

'Alright, Mark?'

I felt my breath release when I recognised the voice. It was Bevan Shaw, one of the other neighbours.

'All good, Bevan. What're you up to, mate?' His block was across the road and down further, but I knew he did a bit of pest control for the Macklin's, on whose property he now stood. I could see the shape of a rifle by his side.

'Just checkin',' he replied. 'Same as you. Clearing a few rabbits.'

I forced a chuckle, his vague response not sitting right with me. 'Can't let these beasts get out through a broken fence mate,' I said, 'I'd hate to see my steaks running down the road.'

It wasn't a great joke and he didn't laugh. My sixth sense hadn't eased off though, and I felt horribly vulnerable standing there with Archie at my side. There was an awkward silence for a moment.

'So you heard the news then,' Bevan finally said. It wasn't a question and his tone was gruff.

'Yeah we did,' I said carefully. 'Not great, eh?'

He grunted.

'You going to be okay?' I said. I figured that talking couldn't hurt right now.

He ignored the question. 'S'pose you heard about it first,' he said, more of an edge in his voice now.

My warning bells were going for it now, clanging in my head like a church steeple in a hurricane.

'How's that?' I said. There was no way he could know my brother worked for Parliamentary Services.

'Huh. You bein' a cop an' that,' he said. 'S'pose you all got told first so you could get...you know...organise your shit and that.'

I didn't appreciate him swearing in front of Archie, but it wasn't the best time to call him on it. I gave a short shake of the head.

'No mate, and I'm not a cop anymore, remember? So even if that did happen I wouldn't have been told. And I doubt it happened anyway.'

He gave another grunt and shuffled his feet. 'Well I'm ready,' he said. 'And better be no shitbirds come beggin' for help when the shit hits the fan.' He hefted his rifle in his hands. 'I'll fuck 'em up.'

Archie looked at me, picking up on Bevan's demeanour.

'Right,' I said. 'We've gotta crack on and get some dinner organised. We'll catch ya later, Bevan.'

'Sure,' he said, and began to move off.

I moved at an angle to keep him in my peripheral vision, and shielded Archie with my body. I got nothing but bad vibes from the man, and it felt reassuring to rest my hand on the concealed butt of the Browning in my waistband.

'He's a strange man, Dad,' Archie said. 'And he's not very happy.'

'No, he's not,' I agreed. I could see Bevan heading back towards the road, hopefully no longer concerned with us. I whistled for Jethro and he galloped over to us, still full of beans.

I'd never had a problem with him before, but Bevan was not someone I considered a friend.

The fact that he was on Macklin's property wouldn't normally concern me, but today it did. His whole demeanour was all off.

And more than anything else, I'd never seen anyone use an AR15 for rabbit hunting before.

20

People jam-packed the station, despite the handwritten sign at the entrance stating that all trains were cancelled.

A train manager was trying to usher people out, loudly telling them that there was no point waiting as the power was out and no trains would be running. Her efforts were in vain, and Gemma wasted no time mucking around.

She turned and steered Alex back out towards the road, struggling to force their way back through the crowd. The footpath was packed as well and nobody was giving an inch.

'Excuse me, excuse me.' She tried to wriggle her way through, Alex tight up behind her, fighting the irritation she felt at people's ignorance.

They had just made it to the footpath when she became aware of pushing behind her, the crowd moving like a wave, bodies pressing and rolling with an unseen current. She felt the weight of people weaving off-balance and elbows and hands started to work as people fought for room. Panic began to rise in her chest as the pressure built, people shouting and shoving all around her.

Gemma stumbled, unable to keep her feet beneath her, and felt herself falling against the bodies crushing around her. She wanted to scream but it was hard enough to even breathe. An elbow clocked her in the side of the head and she felt hands tearing at her day pack, yanking her further off balance.

She tried to turn but stumbled again. Somebody pushed her back and she twisted, getting her feet set, seeing Alex behind her. He was grappling with a bearded guy who had one hand on Gemma's day pack and one hand in Alex's face, pushing him away. He was swearing and shoving and she could see that he easily had the better of Alex. The mass of bodies rolled again and they went with it, stumbling towards the road.

Alex had his face twisted away to escape the guy's fingers, but he was managing to hold onto his opponent's shirt front. There was nothing Gemma could do to help him right now – it was all she could do to stay upright, but the guy holding her bag wasn't helping that either. The mass of bodies reached the road and began to break up, releasing the pressure.

Gemma pushed away from those around her, seeing a few people trip and fall as they came free from the crowd. One woman was holding a baby in a front-carry sling and she went down to one knee, huddling over the baby as people blindly staggered and bumped around her. A man tried to help her up but was knocked down by the crowd.

Gemma was jerked backwards by her bag and she staggered to regain her balance, holding onto her carry bag with one hand and flailing with her other arm. She turned to see that Alex was still being held at arm's length by the guy, the hand in Alex's face having caused a nosebleed. The guy was scratching at her companion's eyes and Alex was twisting away, stuck in a stalemate. She'd had enough of this.

Shrugging her right arm free of the strap, Gemma gave herself more room and pushed away from the people surging past her. She lashed out at the guy, catching him with a decent slap across the cheek.

'Leave him alone!' she shouted.

The guy turned and gave her a surprised look, then removed his hand from Alex's face. He used it to belt Gemma across the side of the head instead, knocking her sideways and down to one knee. Satisfied, he turned back to Alex.

Gemma shook her head and put a hand to the tender spot, cursing. There was no going back now, and she wasn't giving up her bag for this jerk. She started to rise, but realised she was kneeling almost in front of the guy now, his body partially shielding her from the movement of the crowd. He had his legs braced apart as he wrestled with Alex, leaving his groin vulnerable.

Enough was enough. Mark had always told her that if she had to strike, to go for three areas – eyes, throat and nuts.

Gemma sucked in a breath and threw all her might into a straight right jab, burying her fist in the crotch of the guy's jeans. She heard a gasping squeal from above her and he immediately moved. She gave it a second shot, feeling a satisfying squish against her knuckles as she hit home. Her bag came free and she pushed up, getting space from him. He was clutching at his jewels and had no interest in either of them now.

'Come on!'

She grabbed Alex's arm and dragged him along, shoving her way through the crowd towards open space. They kept going until they were clear of the stream of people, and couldn't see the bag snatcher anymore. Gemma pulled up by a fence and put her day pack back on properly, securing the waist and chest straps while Alex dabbed gingerly at his nose with a handkerchief.

Aside from a few bumps and scrapes neither of them was injured, and Gemma thanked her lucky stars they'd escaped unscathed. She'd heard of people being crushed to death in football crowds overseas or at concerts, and that was what it had felt like in there – uncontrolled panic.

They each took a moment to suck down some water before getting set to go again.

'So,' Alex said, putting away his bloodied hankie, 'I guess the trains are out.'

'Looks like it. I think we're walking.'

21

It was an hour of impatience before the tailback got moving again, and even then it was a long, slow process.

The black smoke was easing off but still filled the cab of the motorhome with an oily stench, and after another hour and a half of bumper to bumper crawling they reached the site of the hold up. It was a five-car crash, looking like a head on between two cars and a pile-up of the other three. One car was still burning in the middle of the lane, one was on its roof on the opposite side of the highway, two were mashed nose to tail nearby and the last one was in the ditch at the side.

The road surface was covered in shattered glass and plastic and pieces of debris, and several cars had stopped at the shoulder. People were standing around talking. As they crawled past, Rob could see the people there were in shock. He could see someone lying at the side of the road, unmoving under a blanket. A couple of others were leaning against parked cars, freshly patched up. An older man was sitting down, gingerly holding his ribs.

There was not an emergency services vehicle of any sort in sight.

'Where the hell is everyone?' Sandy wondered aloud. 'Where's the ambulance?'

'I don't think they're coming,' Rob said quietly. He eased the campervan past the scene, avoiding the eyes of the people standing there. He tipped his hat to them for helping, but he had no desire to do so himself. He had others to worry about, not least of all the girl beside him.

Picking up speed once they were clear of the crash, they drove in silence, the hum of the tyres filling the void instead. Rob was seriously worried now – any other day, a crash like that would have had all the emergency services rolling out and people would have been getting attended to.

Help. It was rapidly becoming obvious that there wasn't any.

He leaned over and turned on the radio. Their usual easy listening station was all static, so he started scanning through the frequencies. More of the same, bursts of white noise that told the same story. Nobody was out there.

Exhausting all the FM stations, he flicked over to AM and did the same. The second station he hit was a talkback station that he liked – although he knew it broadcast on both AM and FM, the radio hadn't picked up the FM band.

The announcer wasn't a voice that he recognised. It sounded like she wasn't working from a script, and Rob figured perhaps she wasn't even an announcer. Maybe a producer or someone from behind the scenes.

'...very little information is trickling in but I can tell you that, looking out the window here in downtown Auckland, I can see a lot of smoke and hear a lot of sirens. It looks like there's a lot of fires out there and I've heard there may be a rupture in the gas lines somewhere in the city...as you can imagine, following the announcement from the Beehive, people have been very eager to get home and out of the city, and it's just gridlocked out there. I've never seen anything like it before, I mean we're talking a wet Friday night in the middle of winter with roadworks, but about ten times worse. The cars are not moving at all. I've been watching the same line of cars down there for more than an hour and they haven't moved an inch.'

Sandy glanced across at Rob. 'I hope Gemma's got out already.'

'She got the message same as us,' he said with a confidence he didn't feel. 'She'll be okay.'

'I can see cars have broken down, there's at least two I can see from up here that look like they've overheated and pulled off to the side. Now, we're not getting anything official from the Beehive, no change to the messaging there in the last couple of hours, in fact no contact at all. If anyone has anything solid they can give us, and we're talking facts here, not speculation, please let us know.'

'Good luck with that,' Rob muttered, a sinking feeling in his gut.

'I know that the power is out in some parts of the city, I don't know what that's related to, but it's quite possible that we'll lose the power at some stage here too, so don't be surprised if you lose us all of a sudden.'

'I'd say the power's out in Wellington,' Sandy said. 'From the earthquakes.'

'Could be,' Rob agreed. 'Hopefully it's localised and not just the whole grid.'

The announcer continued on in the background, and it was a few more minutes until Rob's ears pricked up again at the excitement in her voice.

'I can see it from here...people are breaking into shops down here. A guy has just thrown a rubbish bin through the front window of a shop, I think it's an electronics store but I don't have a good angle... yep, someone's just come out with a TV...oh my God, these people are looting the store. They're actually looting it...'

'Fat lot of good a TV is, with no power,' Sandy said.

'I can't believe what I'm seeing here...and they're doing the same at the next store too...oh my Lord, this is something I never thought I'd see in our streets. And there's not a police officer in sight...'

Rob glanced sideways at his wife. 'I dunno why that surprises her,' he said.

'Which part of it, the looting or the fact there's no cops around?'

'Either.'

Rob continued to half listen as he drove, but his mind was bouncing between a hundred different things. The news on the radio certainly hadn't surprised him, but if anything, it had reinforced one thing to him.

Things were turning to shit fast, and nobody was coming to help.

22

I had been listening to the radio in the afternoon, scanning carefully between channels to try and find a broadcast.

Problem was, the atmospherics in our area weren't great and it was hard to get a decent reception at the best of times. And today was definitely not the best of times. After a frustrating hour or so I switched the radio off and put it away again. I went to the kitchen and turned on the hot tap to fill a pot. It was nearly time to get dinner sorted.

The water was lukewarm. My heart sank as I tried the cold tap too – it was fine. The laundry taps were the same. I flicked the light switch and nothing happened. A check of the fuse box in the hallway showed me that nothing had tripped.

'Shit,' I muttered. I don't know if I was more pissed off that the power was out or that I hadn't anticipated it earlier.

I found my mum and Archie on the deck, sitting in the late afternoon sun and watching the heifers grazing in the paddock. Jethro was sprawled at their feet and the cat, Pepper, was on Mum's lap. It was a picture of rural domesticity and I was about to break the magic.

Thinking better of it, I backed inside and set about getting torches and lamps out. That done, I filled a large pot with cold water and set it on the barbecue, ready to boil for washing dishes later.

I cracked on with dinner and soon the beef stir fry I'd prepared for the frying pan was sizzling on the barbecue. I tossed a pack of Udon noodles through it and flavoured it with a good dose of my homemade sauce, leaving aside a no-sauce portion for Archie. He wasn't as worldly with his tastes just yet and was happy to add good old-fashioned tomato sauce to pretty much anything.

I served the food in bowls and we sat around the dining table inside, eating in the fading light with candles flickering. Archie thought it was pretty cool that the power was off but I could tell my mother wasn't so sure.

'Don't worry Grandma,' Archie told her, 'we've got a spare torch for you. It'll be fun.'

She managed a smile, but I could see the strain in her face. It was nothing compared to what was going on inside me.

There had been no messages on my phone, so I didn't know where the McMasters were or what they were doing. I hadn't heard back from Gemma's sister, Carla. I couldn't get online because the connection was down. My outgoing messages were backed up waiting to send, so I couldn't update anyone or give them a hurry-up.

Now the power was out and it was getting dark and Gemma wasn't home.

23

Barely ten minutes after clearing the scene of the big crash, the McMasters were brought to a halt in another tailback.

This one extended as far as the eye could see, and Rob wasted no time in killing the engine. No point in burning gas for nothing. They sat in silence while he checked the road map he kept in the glove box. Unlike GPS, a road map had never let him down.

'We're about here,' he reckoned, marking a spot with his finger. 'As the crow flies, we're probably only about fifteen, twenty k's away.'

'How long by road?' Sandy asked, twisting to see the map.

'Normal driving, should take us about twenty minutes, if that.'

Sandy sighed. 'Well I can't see this lot moving very fast.'

'We might be here a while,' he agreed.

A noticeable smell of petrol was wafting through the air con and he closed off the nearest vent. He ran his eye over the map, looking for a side road they could take. There was one a few k's back that took a meandering route towards their destination, or up ahead a couple more kilometres was another.

With the traffic jammed up like it was there was no way to get ahead except up the shoulder of the road, but already he could see at least one broken down car pulled off to the side, blocking their way. The median barrier prevented a U-turn to get back around.

Rob stifled a sigh and sat back to wait, just settling in when the sound of an approaching motorbike reached him. He spotted a road bike weaving its way back through the twin lines of traffic, coming towards him. The rider was taking their time, pausing every so often to speak to motorists.

Rob climbed down from the motorhome and waited, waving to the biker as he approached. The bike pulled up and the rider lifted his helmet visor. He was riding a sleek red Kawasaki.

'What's the hold up?' Rob said, stepping closer so he could hear. A surprising number of the vehicles around them were still idling, and exhaust fumes wafted about.

'A fuel tanker's flipped,' the guy said, his voice muffled by his helmet. 'The whole road's covered in gas, about three k's up. It really stinks.'

'And there's no way to get over the other side?'

The biker shook his head. 'Na. There's a side road before it but there's been a couple of nose-to-tails and the traffic's going nowhere. Plus a couple of breakdowns. Nobody can get through.'

'No traffic cops or fire service?'

'None.' The guy patted his handlebars. 'Lucky I'm on a bike; you guys aren't goin' anywhere.'

'What's it like back behind us?' Rob said.

'Dunno mate, haven't got there yet.'

Rob sensed the guy wanted to get going, but he needed information and this guy could be the key to getting it.

'You reckon you could do us a favour?' he asked.

The guy's eyes flattened. 'Depends. I've gotta get home mate.'

'I appreciate that, and it won't take long. That side road back a wee ways; you reckon you could zip down and see if there's a way we can get back to it?'

The biker hesitated.

'I'd really appreciate it if you could.' Rob indicated the motorhome behind him and laid it on thick. 'The wife's not well, y'know, I don't think the stress is doing her any good and I could really do with getting her home, y'know?'

He could see the resignation in the guy's eyes. 'I'll be back shortly.'

The bike eased off and Rob felt a lift in his spirits. It seemed to be an age before the bike came back and when it did, the biker wasn't wasting any time. He manoeuvred around to face back the way he'd come and lifted his visor.

'Traffic behind you is jammed up, there's a three car crash a k back. Some arsehole knocked a motorbike over and the rider's not looking good.' The anger in the guy's tone was clear. 'I can't see it getting cleared any time soon, but if it is and people start backing up, you could eventually get back to that side road and turn off, okay?'

Rob nodded. 'Got it. Thanks mate, I appreciate your help.'

'Good luck.' The guy gave him a thumbs up and moved off.

Rob climbed back into the cab, getting an enquiring look from Sandy.

'Settle in,' he said. 'Looks like we're probably here for the night.'

24

By the time Gemma and Alex entered Cornwall Park it was close to dusk, and they were both tired and stressed and in need of rest.

In the fading light they saw the odd person or small group, and the roads within the park were still heavily lined with cars. The car parks were more than half full and it appeared that some vehicles were providing temporary accommodation for the night.

'A lot of people can't get home, I s'pose,' Alex said. 'Maybe we should've stayed with Teri after all.'

'What, and miss all this fun?' Gemma tried to inject some humour into her voice, but she was hungry and thirsty and her feet hurt.

'Where are we staying, anyway? Have you got a tent in there?'

Gemma stepped off the roadway and crossed to a fence at the base of the mountain. It barely warranted the title, One Tree *Hill* seeming far more appropriate. Like many, she and her family had walked the park and hill numerous times, had picnics and flown kites and kicked balls around on the wide green fields. She knew the park well enough to know where she would feel safest for the night.

'Over here.' She climbed the fence and waited for him to join her.

Alex looked dubiously at the sheep he could see past her. 'What about them?'

'I'm pretty sure they don't bite.'

Gemma led the way. The paddock they had entered was part of the rocky foothills, full of hillocks and crevices and gullies, home to the sheep that were cared for by the park rangers as well as rabbits and possums and who knew what else. Gnarly trees were dotted about.

Once they were out of sight of the road, Gemma stopped and scanned. The bottom of the gully would probably be boggy and wet, so she climbed a small hillock and found an area near some bushes that was flat enough and seemed dry and sheltered.

'This is us,' she said.

Dropping his bag, Alex took out a water bottle and drained it. He looked exhausted and his nose was puffy. He put his empty bottle away and watched as Gemma took a folded green tarp from her bag. She spread it out and rummaged in her carry bag, this time producing the tow rope she'd taken from the car.

'Here.' She passed him an end of the rope and stepped back, unravelling it.

Alex looked around him. 'Where do I tie it?'

'The bushes beside you,' Gemma said, busy looping her end around the trunk of a rotted tree that had fallen. 'No, on the trunk.' She watched him trying to figure it out for a moment, wondering how often he actually left the computer rooms. 'No no no...Alex, the twig will break. Reach in and find the trunk or a solid branch...tie it off there.'

His voice was muffled because he'd buried his head in the bush.

'Right over left, left over right...' she said. 'Don't do it too tight, but make sure it's secure.'

More muffled muttering before he emerged, straightening his glasses. A leaf was stuck in his hair and she would have laughed if he hadn't looked so pissed off.

'This is bullshit,' he grumbled.

'It is bullshit,' she agreed. 'It's bullshit that we're not home with our families, that's what's bullshit.'

In normal circumstances there was no way she would share a sleeping area with a guy she hardly knew, but things were different now. Right now, she figured there was safety in numbers. Her gut told her that Alex was safe, and she had always trusted her gut.

The smell of smoke was strong on the breeze and she guessed that fires were still burning in the city – hopefully not closer. There were a couple of dust masks in her bag but they hadn't needed them yet.

With Gemma giving the directions, they soon had the tarp set up as an A-frame shelter, pegged out at the sides. She put down the boot liner from her carry bag as a groundsheet and spread the picnic blanket on top of it. It wouldn't be the most comfortable of beds but at least they would be insulated from the cold ground.

Dusk was on them by the time they finished and the temperature was dropping.

'Hungry?' Gemma said, crouching down beside their shelter and opening her bag.

'Starving. Got any marshmallows in there? I reckon I could build a fire.'

Gemma doubted that, although the thought of a fire was appealing. 'Sorry, no. I could do a can of creamed rice?'

Alex's face lit up. 'Yum. My Mum makes a mean creamed rice pudding. She puts sultanas and cinnamon and stuff in it, it's awesome.'

'Well this is just a can,' Gemma said. 'Chocolate flavoured and it's cold. Sorry.'

She handed him the can with a spoon.

'What're you having?' Alex sat cross-legged beside her and ripped the top off the can.

Gemma peered at the bar in her hand. 'Chocolate fudge protein bar,' she said. 'Probably tastes like arse.'

Alex snorted into his mouthful of rice and chuckled. 'Tastes like arse...'

They ate in silence, each lost in their thoughts as they processed the day they'd just experienced. Gemma wondered for the millionth time what was happening home. Were Mark and Archie safe? Her parents?

From what she'd seen so far, things were turning to shit fast. It surprised her how quickly people had gone feral. Big Nick in the car park at work, the people at the train station. Such behaviour was not normal, but she knew it was not far from the surface for some people.

Being married to a cop for so long had given her many insights into human nature. When normal people discussed their day at work, they talked about meeting deadlines, or the copier breaking down, or restructures.

Mark's work discussions revolved around dead bodies, violence and abuse, and the dregs of society. Lives destroyed by soulless beings who cared for nothing but themselves. Brazen acts of violence or theft by thugs who saw it all as theirs for the taking. He was constantly on the lookout, watching people around them, paranoid about the safety of his family, looking for the ulterior motives behind everything.

All of this had rubbed off on Gemma, who was exposed to it for so long that inevitably some of his habits became hers. She always found herself less trusting than her friends and colleagues, more conscious of her personal security. She was aware that it sometimes took the shine off things, but in other ways it paid dividends. She was always the one who parked in well-lit areas, never walked alone at night, and automatically assessed every person she met.

Perhaps with things the way they were such an approach would keep her safe.

Gemma stuck the empty wrapper in her bag and dug out a head-lamp. She handed Alex the spare torch from the car.

'I'm going to the toilet.' She pointed behind the shelter. 'That way. I'll be back in a minute.' The message in her voice was clear.

'Sure thing.' He nodded. 'I'll guard the castle.'

Peeing behind a bush was not a new experience, but today it felt different. Everything felt different. By the time Gemma was back at the shelter Alex had got himself ready. He'd put on his hoody and folded his bag into a makeshift pillow and sat with his knees up, like a kid waiting for instructions.

Gemma took a silver emergency blanket and a thin nylon poncho from her bag, and handed them to him. 'Here, try and keep warm.'

He took them without protest, and watched as she pulled on her thermal top, rain jacket and beanie. She unfolded the ugly car seat blanket.

'Are you always like this?' he asked suddenly.

'Ready for bed early?'

'No...prepared. Calm.'

Gemma surprised herself by laughing. 'Calm? I'm not calm, Alex, I'm just trying to get home.'

'Well you're a lot calmer than I am right now.'

She paused and looked at him. The torchlight threw long shadows around them. 'Hey, we'll be fine. We just need to stick together and watch each other's backs, like we did today. You did good with that guy at the train station; he would've got my bag if you hadn't been there.'

'You punched him in the nuts.'

'True, but if I'd been on my own I'd have been in real trouble with him. Stop doubting yourself.'

She crawled into the shelter and arranged the blanket. Alex waited for her to get organised before he followed suit.

'You put your head that end,' Gemma told him, 'and I'll go this end.'

She lay on half of the blanket and pulled the other half over her, resting her head on her bag. It was far from comfortable but at least they were sheltered from any wind and rain, and were as warm as she could hope for.

The darkness was complete once the lights were off, the kind of complete darkness you only got in the wild. It was hard to believe they were still in the city.

Gemma closed her eyes and took deep breaths. There were many things that were hard to believe today.

25

The first I knew of visitors was the sound of feet crunching on the gravel driveway.

I sat up with a jolt, unaware that I had even fallen asleep. The Rossi was across my lap and in seconds I was standing to the side of the ranch slider, the rifle in my hands. The moon was hiding behind a cloud so it was almost pitch-black outside, only the stars above giving some slight illumination. Jethro had padded into the lounge from his usual sleeping spot outside Archie's door, and stood beside me, a low growl in his throat.

It took a few more seconds to get my bearings but when I did, I saw them.

Two dark figures were standing at the top of the drive, looking towards the house. Either scoping or waiting; it didn't matter which, the bastards were on my property and that was a situation that needed to change.

I backed carefully away from the doors, confident that they couldn't see me unless they had night vision goggles. I moved through the house, pausing at the hallway to listen. Nothing.

'Jethro, stay,' I whispered. I didn't want to be tripping over him in the dark. He didn't like it, but he stayed guard inside the house.

The back door opened silently and I padded along the side of the house to the turning area. The night air was cool on my skin and I could hear stealthy footsteps coming my way. Stealthy, that is, aside from the crunch of gravel.

I waited silently, my mouth half open so I could hear better. The footsteps stopped a few metres away, followed by a whispered conversation. The problem with whispering when you want to be covert is that it sounds unnatural, so you're better off talking in low tones. Whispers are squeaky and audible.

I could easily hear these two clowns, and both sounded like uneducated thugs.

'Check the door, bro.'

'Ow, gimme the torch, I can't see.'

'Don't turn it on G, someone'll see it.'

There was a flicker of light around the corner of the house.

'Ow fuck G, what're you doing?'

'I can't see, bro. It's too dark.'

'Fuck bro, you're a egg. Turn it off or I'll fuckin' slap you, G.'

I had heard enough. These weren't lost travellers looking for help. In one swift move I stepped around the corner of the house, lighting them up with the LED torch duct-taped under the barrel.

They both reeled back, trying to block the blinding light with their arms. A pair of scruffy Maori boys, late teens, one with a gang bandanna hanging from the waist of his low-slung jeans. The one holding their torch dropped it in fright and let out a squeal.

'Get your fuckin' hands up,' I snarled. Four hands shot skywards and they automatically dropped their heads away from the light.

'Ow, turn it off bro,' one of them whined. 'I can't see.'

'You could see well enough to come on my property and try to break in,' I said. 'So you can see well enough to get the fuck off it again.'

'We weren't even breaking in, G,' the other one said. 'We're looking for our uncle's place.'

'Bullshit. Turn around and get walking.'

The mouthier one started to lower his hands, trying to look defiant.

'Or what?' His tone was challenging.

There was a round in the chamber but I levered the action anyway, popping out the unused round. There's nothing more intimidating than the *clack-clack* of a gun being racked.

'Or I'll blow your fuckin' arse away,' I told him, 'and no one will bat an eye.'

The second guy had jumped with fright and put his hands out, as if they were going to stop a load of lead.

'Don't shoot,' he was whining, 'ow mister, don't shoot! I ain't even got a gun!'

The leader was the stauncher of the two, but he started to back up. They began to move back towards the driveway and I stayed several metres away, wary of being jumped. I had made my mind up; if they had a crack, I would drop them.

We got to the drive and I herded them down, the torch lighting the way. I could hear the animals in the paddocks, probably disturbed by the unexpected activity at night. The two boys kept walking, the leader gradually lowering his hands as he went.

'Keep your hands up, shithead.'

'Ow, you all tough coz you got a gun eh.' He made a scoffing sound. 'What a fuckin' egg, G.'

'Hey boy.'

He turned around and I hooked him in the face with a good left. He staggered back, putting a hand to his face and cursing. I trained the Rossi back on his chest, the torch blinding him.

'I'm not tough because I've got a gun,' I said. 'And I'm not your G, dickhead. Keep walking.'

I followed them to the end of the drive and out to the road. The road was empty.

'How'd you get here?'

'Up around the corner,' the second guy said. 'Got a car.'

'Go.'

They moved off again, both with their hands in the air. We

reached the next road and I saw an old Subaru with primer paint on one door half off the road.

'Stop there.' They stopped and half turned towards me. I kept the gun up. 'You pricks get something in your head. Things are turning to shit right now, and you think that means you've got free reign to go thieving and do what the fuck you want, right?'

Neither of them said anything. I took their silence as agreement.

'What it really means is that people have to look after their own shit. So take me. I'm a normal dude. I don't go looking for trouble. But if trouble comes looking for me?' I let out a low whistle. 'By Jesus, trouble better be ready for a scrap, because I am.'

I let that sink in for a moment.

'How many eyes do you think are on you right now?'

The second guy gave a small shrug; I could tell he was listening properly.

'Trust me, I'm not alone here. And the others around here? None of them will give a fuck if I blow you away right now. So this is your one and only chance; get the fuck outta here and don't come back. If I see you back here again then it's open season. Understand?'

The second guy nodded his agreement. The leader stayed staunch, but nodded anyway.

'Where are you boys from?'

'Meremere,' the second guy said without hesitation.

I knew the place. Further south, off State Highway One, it was a shit-box town with plenty of state housing and fuck-all going for it. Thieves from Meremere were transient between there and south Auckland, and it had a strong gang element. It didn't surprise me that they were already taking advantage of the situation.

'You got five seconds,' I told them. 'If you're still here then I'll start shooting.'

They started edging away.

'Go!'

They ran for the car. It took longer than five seconds but they took off with a wheel spin and a spray of dirt and gravel, and I stayed where I was until I could no longer hear the car.

I killed the torch and stood in the silence, catching my breath. I could feel sweat on my back and under my arms. I hated gangsters and I hated the fact they had violated our property.

I was happy that they had gone, but the question was, would they return?

26

Dawn was finally breaking when Gemma prodded Alex's shoulder. He stirred, scrunched up like a child, and kept his eyes shut.

'Alex, time to get up.'

When he finally opened his eyes he saw her kneeling beside him. She was fully dressed and her bag was strapped closed, ready to go.

'Bloody hell,' he muttered, rolling over gingerly and yawning. 'Did you even go to sleep?'

'Barely. Maybe an hour or two all up.'

She didn't want to tell him that while he was snoring away she had stirred at every noise, every change in temperature, every minute movement in the air. Her body ached from the exertions of the day before and from the cold, hard ground. She was hungry and thirsty and felt like she'd been hit by a bus.

While Alex fluffed about getting himself ready she took down the bivvy and folded the tarps. To free herself from carrying a bag in her hand, she used a bungy to secure the rolled tarps to her day pack. She folded the two blankets and put them with the torch and rope beside Alex's bag, letting him know he could carry them today.

She rinsed her mouth out and drank some more water. She had

started yesterday with three 500mL bottles, and two were now empty. She would need to find a water source today and refill to avoid dehydrating. The food supplies were also nearly gone. She knew a person could last three days without water and three weeks without food, but she had no plans to test that theory.

Gemma left Alex to sort out his own gear while she stretched her legs and walked around, trying to ease some of the stiffness that had set in overnight. She could hear the sheep in the paddock some distance away, and smelt smoke in the air. She could hear Alex urinating on leaves behind a tree, sighing to himself. She guessed he wasn't a morning person.

She rolled her shoulders, hearing a crack in her neck, wondering what Mark and Archie were doing. Hopefully they were safely asleep and not stressing about her, although she knew they would be.

She would give anything to cuddle her little boy right now. She felt her eyes prickling as she thought about him; she knew he would be missing her, even though he was in safe hands with Mark.

She swallowed hard, determined to hold her composure. She had cried enough in the night; no need to continue now when she needed to focus.

'We need to get home,' she said, turning to Alex.

He was putting his day pack on and nodded. 'I'm ready.'

'Here.' She held out half a Snickers bar to him. 'Don't forget your breakfast.'

He gave a wry smile and took it. 'Thanks.'

They set off with Gemma in the lead, the grey dawn giving enough light to make their way back to the road and follow that through the park. She noticed that some of the vehicles parked up had fogged windows, a sure sign that people had bunked there for the night. She wondered if any of them were equipped in any way for such an outing.

She saw a young couple moving around beside a campervan decked out with hire company signage and a flag that she didn't recognise. She caught a sweet, pungent smell in the air and saw the guy puffing on a small pipe. They both looked warily at her and

Alex as they passed nearby. She gave them a short nod and kept walking.

The trees were dropping their leaves and the park was a blaze of colour. Autumn was definitely here. Archie loved playing in the leaves, rolling around and throwing them in the air with the carefree abandonment of the young. Just the thought of it gave Gemma a spur to keep going.

Passing the large gas barbecues in the picnic area, Gemma noticed a drink fountain and they stopped to refill their bottles. She took a long drink herself and washed her face, the cold water shocking her skin into life. She waited while Alex did the same, keeping watch for any unwanted visitors.

They walked in silence to the edge of the park and took a path between houses out to the street. What was normally a busy thoroughfare at any time of the day was almost empty. There were cars parked outside some of the houses, and there was a taxi van smashed into the side of a sedan in the middle of an intersection further along. Broken glass was scattered around the collision site and a random single sneaker lay nearby.

Gemma took stock of their surroundings, realising after a few moments that despite the apparent quiet of the neighbourhood, people were in fact up and about. Lights glowed in some windows and she saw the odd person moving around their property. A siren yelped somewhere in the distance.

She didn't need to check the map just yet – the short-term aim was to head south towards Manukau. The most direct route would be to cross the Manukau Harbour from Onehunga to Mangere Bridge, which would carry them on through Otahuhu and Papatoetoe. She knew they were high crime areas and wanted to avoid them if possible.

The slightly longer but probably less risky option was to cut east towards the motorway. Beyond that was Ellerslie, Mount Wellington and Otara. From there they could drop straight down into Manukau where Alex would hopefully make it home.

They had discussed it briefly last night and tried to work out a plan of attack, but Alex didn't have a strong opinion either way and seemed happy for Gemma to make the decisions. At least that gave her some freedom but she wasn't entirely happy with carrying all the responsibility either. This was more Mark's thing than hers; she had the feeling he would've been in his element, planning then executing their escape from the city.

Gemma wasn't sure that she was the right person for this situation, but she did know that right now the best thing they could do was to keep moving. Every step they took was one step closer to home. With that in mind, she broke from the cover of the walkway and crossed the street. Alex trotted behind her and she gave him an encouraging smile when he joined her on the footpath.

'You okay?' she said.

He nodded and hitched his bag on his shoulders. He looked cold and tired and unhappy. Gemma gave him another smile, hoping to boost his spirits; she didn't have the time or energy to babysit him if he was going to be a sad sack.

'Cool,' she said, 'let's go. We've got some miles to make.'

She headed along the footpath, feeling they would be safest staying on the main roads. They quickly hit Great South Road, the main arterial that ran from the fringe of the central city all the way down to the Bombay hills. If they stayed on that the whole way, she knew it would take them where they needed to go. Problem was it ran through built up areas all the way past Papakura, and her gut told her that they were likely to strike trouble the longer this went on.

Built-up areas might not be safe for very long.

As if to emphasise her point she heard the roar of a car engine approaching behind them and she spun, seeing a lowered Holden V8 flying towards the Great South Rd intersection at a rate of knots. It was tinted out and had damage to the front right, and a Police patrol car was some way behind it – she could hear the siren now and the flashing red and blues were lighting up the dawn.

'Watch out,' she called out to Alex, stepping back against the front hedge of the house on the corner.

The Holden came up fast, slowed marginally as it approached the intersection then threw a right turn, the back of the car fishtailing wildly. It clipped the far kerb outside a new car dealership and bounced, the tyres smoked and it took off again. The Police car took the corner much slower and she she could see two cops in it. The siren was deafeningly loud. The passenger had the radio mic to her mouth and the driver looked tense.

The Police car barrelled after the Holden and Gemma glanced back to check on Alex. As she did so she heard two sounds simultaneously; the screech of brakes and the crack of gunshots. She whirled and pressed herself back into the hedge.

The Police car had slid to a stop in the middle of the road, its siren still blaring and the lights still flashing. Thirty or so metres ahead of them the blacked-out Holden had slewed across the road and Gemma could see three guys standing near it. One had a rifle of some sort at the shoulder and the guy beside him had a short-barrelled weapon braced against his hip. The third was watching and yelling something unintelligible.

The two cops were bailing out and the two gunmen were firing at them. She recognised the throaty boom of a shotgun and realised the short-barrelled weapon was probably a sawn-off shotgun. The rifle had a lighter crack.

'What the hell is that?' Alex appeared beside her, stepping out into the open and staring at the scene unfolding before them. 'Oh fuck!'

He threw himself back against the hedge, his eyes wide. The police car was taking rounds even as the two cops were burrowing in the boot, trying to slide open the gun drawer that was there.

Gemma watched the girl cop grab a holstered pistol and attach it to the clip on her belt then draw the weapon and rack it. The guy got his hands on a Bushmaster M4 and in a couple of seconds was leaning round the back of the car, putting rounds down towards the guys at the Holden.

'What the hell are we going to do?' Alex panted. His eyes were wide and his face had gone several shades lighter than normal.

Gemma could feel her heart slamming against her ribcage.

Things had taken a sudden turn for the worst and the plan she had worked out only moments ago had just flown out the window. She played for time, taking a moment to glance around the corner. Bullets were flying in both directions and she could hear impacts against both cars.

As she watched, the male cop leaned out from behind the patrol car with his rifle at the shoulder, trying for a better angle. She saw his body jerk and he fell backwards, flat on his back on the roadway.

'Jesus,' Gemma whispered to herself, clapping a hand to her mouth. She saw the cop struggle to get up, fall back and push himself up again. He was hit again and this time she saw a spray of blood. He hit the deck again and his legs twitched.

The female cop began to move, rising up to pop a couple of shots at the guys behind the blacked-out car, then shuffling round the patrol car towards her partner. She reached the end of her cover and was yelling at him. Gemma knew there would be no answer, and the female cop seemed to realise too.

Holstering her pistol, she lunged forward and grabbed him by the arm, trying to drag him back into cover. A second later she was knocked sideways and hit the deck in an awkward sitting position, screaming blue murder.

Gemma ducked back around the corner, bumping into Alex. 'They just shot those cops! OhmyfuckingGod!'

Alex let out a squeal and his eyes bugged. Gemma grabbed him by the front of his shirt. 'Shhh! Shut up!'

'What're we gunna do? Fuck fuck fuck!'

'Shut up!' Gemma risked another peek around the corner, half expecting to see the bad guys coming towards them. All three of them were standing over the two fallen cops now, their guns pointed at them. The female cop was whimpering, clutching onto her leg with one hand, the other hand raised up defensively.

The guy with the sawn-off shotgun raised the stubby barrel slightly and blasted her in the chest at point blank range. She flopped backwards and didn't move. The three guys laughed and the one with the rifle stepped forward, firing a shot into the body of each cop.

Gemma felt her gut go cold and she desperately needed to pee. She stayed frozen where she was, watching as they picked up the discarded M4 rifle and relieved the girl of her holstered Glock. Without looking back the three thugs turned and trotted back to their Holden. Seconds later they were gone, peeling away in a cloud of tyre smoke.

She looked around, realising for the first time that the whole neighbourhood had gone suddenly silent. Not a single car or person could be heard.

'They're gone,' she heard herself say. 'We need to go check on them.'

'We can't go out there!' Alex squealed, grabbing her arm. 'What if they come back?'

Gemma shook him off. 'And what if those cops are still alive? My husband was a cop – they could be people he knew.' She looked him in the eye, feeling a rush of determination despite her fear. 'Stay here if you want, but I'm going to check on them.'

She didn't hang around to argue.

Neither cop was moving when she got to them, both of them lying in a pool of blood. The girl's chest was an open mass of red and pink flesh and she was staring at the sky, a look of complete terror frozen on her face. The guy was on his side and the pool of blood around him was huge and steadily spreading. He was unmoving.

Knowing there would be a first aid kit in the car, Gemma moved round to the boot of the patrol car. She first saw two sets of body armour lying in the boot beneath the open gun tray, and realised that neither cop had donned it before they engaged the bad guys. Maybe if they hadn't been in such an enforced rush they would have survived. Maybe not.

Her eyes fell to the gun tray and she saw a holstered pistol sitting there in the foam lining. Beside it were two spare magazines in black pouches. She wondered if she should take it. Even though they had guns at home she'd only ever fired a pistol once before, when one of Mark's mates had come over for a shoot-up. It had been an automatic of some sort, a forty-five they had said, and she remembered it kicking when she fired it.

She left the pistol where it was for now and grabbed the red first aid kit below the tray. It was a day pack and felt full. As she was lifting it out she heard Alex shouting at her from behind. She turned and saw the blacked-out Holden flying back up Great South Road towards them. She realised she'd been so absorbed in what she was doing that she'd blocked out her surroundings.

'Oh shit.' Gemma dropped the first aid kit and stared at the approaching car. It was only seconds away from reaching her. Obviously the bad guys had decided to return for some reason; maybe to steal the patrol car, maybe set it on fire. Whatever their reason was it didn't matter. She was here and she was exposed.

She knew instinctively they would have no hesitation in killing her.

27

Gemma snatched up the holstered pistol – Mark always called them Glocks – and tried to draw it.

It was stuck and it took her a moment to find the thumb catch to unlock it. She pushed the hammer strap forward and the Glock cleared the holster at the same time as the bad guys skidded to a halt a few metres away on the other side of the patrol car.

She could hear their voices, rough and uneducated, every second word a swear word. She remembered she had to rack the slide on top of the gun and she pulled it back. It clacked forward loudly and one of the thugs gave a shout.

'Whaddafuck?'

'Eh, who the fuck's 'at?'

Gemma had the pistol in both hands now, remembering to keep her finger outside the trigger guard, and she stepped away from the car so they could see her.

'Get back,' she said as loudly as she could. 'Get back!'

'Eh, what the fuck cunt?' The speaker was the one with the sawn-off shotgun, a fat man with bushy hair and shades on despite the early hour. 'Who the fuck you think you are, bitch? Fuckin' talk to me like that, cunt, I'll fuck you up.'

'I said get back.' Gemma raised the Glock so they could see it clearly, pointing it directly at the speaker.

'Ow, fuck bro!' The guy with the rifle – not the cop's M4 – ducked off to the side, bringing his gun around.

'Fuckin' bitch!' The guy with the sawn-off raised it and in that instant things changed.

Gemma knew without a doubt that she was about to get shot; it was no longer an option to run.

She pulled the trigger without even realising her finger had moved. The pistol bucked in her hand and the guy staggered backwards. His shotgun went off with a roar, blasting out a window on the other side of the patrol car. She had no idea if she'd hit him or not, but she could no longer see him.

Gemma ducked backwards, jerking off another shot that punched a hole in the sky somewhere. The other two guys were scrambling for cover and she took cover herself, getting behind the patrol car and tucking herself in against the rear wheel. Her ears were ringing from the sound of the shots but still her heart was deafeningly loud.

Glass exploded over her from above and she realised the bad guys were shooting at her. She knew that she had to do something, otherwise she was dead.

Peeking up above the door frame brought another shot, the bullet whining off the roof of the patrol car. She ducked back down then immediately up again, bringing the Glock up in both hands at the same time as the guy with the cop's M4 was coming around the back of his car. He was firing towards the patrol car but she was unaware of where his bullets were going.

Gemma squeezed the trigger then, the pistol bucking in her grip. The gunman did a double take and she fired a fourth time, and again and again. He turned and ran back behind the car, shouting to his mate. Gemma kept firing, seeing the side windows crack then shatter as the bullets impacted. She heard a shout from somewhere but ignored it and fired two more shots.

The Holden revved hard and started to move, exposing the guy with the cop's M4. He loosed off another shot at her which exploded the light bar on the roof of the patrol car then dived into the Holden as it took off. Gemma fired again at it as it raced away then straightened up and watched it go.

She licked her lips and tried to swallow but her mouth was like sandpaper. She looked at the Glock in her hands. Blue smoke was curling from the barrel and the slide was locked open. She knew that meant she was out of bullets.

'Well that's lucky,' she heard herself saying, then laughed. It sounded incongruous to be laughing at a time like this but she couldn't help it.

She jumped when she realised Alex was approaching, looking at her as if she were a mad woman.

'Are you okay?' he asked tentatively.

Gemma got herself under control and wiped her face. 'Yeah, sorry. I'm fine.'

'You just shot that guy,' Alex told her.

Gemma nodded, reality coming back with a bang. She had just shot a guy.

'I thought you were going to die,' Alex said. There was a tremor in his voice. 'That was...unreal. Bloody unreal, man.'

Gemma nodded. She didn't know what to say. She put the Glock on the ground and unslung her daypack. In half a minute she had drained a water bottle. She wiped her mouth and stuffed the bottle back into the bag. Then she picked up the spare magazines in their pouches and shoved them into her bag.

'Oh Jesus,' she heard Alex saying. 'Oh Jesus.'

Looking up, she saw the blacked-out Holden flying back up the road towards them.

'Run!' Gemma rammed the Glock into the daypack and slung it on, grabbed the first aid bag and bolted back across the road the way they had come.

They reached the corner and she darted into the first driveway, running through somebody's property to a fence. She hurled the first aid bag over it and climbed onto the rails, hauling herself up.

'Hurry!' Alex dragged himself over after her as doors slammed out on the road and shouts sounded.

'This way!' Gemma dropped to her hands and knees and forced herself through a low gap in a hedge to the next property, shoving the red bag ahead of her. Alex was hard on her heels, panting and gasping.

She was up and running again with the red first aid bag in her hands, the daypack bouncing on her back, and within seconds they were over another fence and gaining distance.

She didn't know what else to do but keep running, so that's what they did.

28

The sun was up by the time I finished my morning tasks.

I had risen early after a night of tossing and turning, my mind racing and churning over the million things I wanted and needed to do. Top of the list was making sure my family was safe.

To that end I had walked our property in the dark, checking the fences and outbuildings for any sign of interference and also any sign of a weak point, then had repeated the process in the grey light of dawn. Jethro joined me for the second lap, happy to get out and have a sniff around. I had the lever action Rossi in my hands and the Browning holstered on my hip in case things went wrong.

Our location was great for what we bought it for, but in the situation the country now found itself I doubted that we were isolated enough for that to be a major strength. To counter that I needed to make sure that our property was both unappealing to any potential intruders and also defensible against those that pushed their luck.

With just myself and my mother home right now it would be a tough task to defend it against a determined foe. On the flip side of that was the fact that most burglars and thieves tend to be gutless scumbags that prey on the weak. The key was to give the impression of strength without fully showing your hand.

The intruders of the previous night caused me concern; we had never had such an incident at this house before, and for it to happen so soon after things turned to shit did not bode well for the future. My hand had been forced into confronting the threat head-on, which had revealed the fact that I was armed and prepared to use force. Should the burglars return they would be forewarned of what they were up against, so I needed to have more plays in my gamebook to counter that.

In normal circumstances I would have said that the likelihood of some shitbag returning to a house where a man stuck a gun in their face was very low, but in the current situation, who knew?

On top of all that I was worried as hell about Gemma. Cell phone connections were down and I didn't know if my texts were going through or, if they were, whether her phone was even charged. She was notoriously slack at keeping it juiced up.

I came back to the house with a plan in mind and a renewed determination. I needed information, and there was only one place to get it.

Archie was up and about when I got inside, sitting at the breakfast bar eating dry Weetbix and drinking milk. He was wearing his monster dressing gown over his racing cars pyjamas and looked small and vulnerable, but his face lit up when he saw me.

'Daddy!'

He jumped down and ran to me for a cuddle. I had placed the weapons in the hall cupboard and just had time to kick off my boots before he got to me. I held him against my chest, his arms wrapped around my neck, cherishing the closeness. He had always been a cuddly kid and Gemma and I were determined to make the most of it before he became a mono-syllabic moody teenager.

We chatted while I prepared a proper breakfast for both of us. He wanted to know what I had been doing outside and I explained, without mentioning the burglars, that I just needed to make sure the animals were okay. He accepted that and hoed into a bowl of Weetbix, fruit and yoghurt. The power was working again but at low strength, so I fired up the gas BBQ on the deck to boil the jug and make toast.

Archie was starting on his jam toast when Grandma appeared. She had clearly slept badly and the redness of her eyes told me she had been crying.

I gave her a hug and when I went to pull away she held on like she had when I was a kid. I knew the feeling now and hugged her back.

'It'll be okay, Mum,' I told her. 'Grab a coffee.'

I poured her a cup while she gave Archie a kiss on the head and a half hug. He did what he needed to do without tearing himself away from his toast.

With a mug of coffee in her hand and the sun shining in the kitchen window she cheered up somewhat. I hadn't told her about the burglars either, knowing she would just stress out, but if I was to leave them at home together, she needed to know. I didn't want to take them into town without knowing what we were heading into.

'Did you get much sleep?' my mother asked, and I gave a shrug. 'She'll be fine,' she continued, giving me one of those motherly looks. 'She'll be home before you know it.'

'No doubt,' I agreed, more for Archie's benefit than my own; I knew that there was little I could do right now to speed up Gemma's return home.

I finished off my coffee and put the mug in the sink. Knowing that my mother was no great fan of my wife, and vice versa, made it uncomfortable to discuss one with the other. I wondered momentarily whether my mother would actually really care if Gemma made it home or not. I knew I couldn't afford to dwell on such negative thoughts, but it was a reality.

'Right,' I said, turning to face them both. 'I have a job for you two today.'

'Am I going to school, Dad?' Archie asked. He had a smear of jam on his cheek and I wiped it away.

'No buddy, not today. Probably not for a few days.'

'Why not? We've got Jump Jam today.'

'I know bud, but school's closed for a few days. The earthquakes down in Wellington have caused quite a few problems, and the Government – the people that run the country – are trying to work out how to fix things so that we can all go on with our normal lives, okay?'

'So I'm not going to school then, like in the school holidays?'

'That's right.' I gave him a reassuring grin, watching as he processed this change of events in his head. 'So that means you get to stay home and do fun stuff instead.'

'And look after Grandma.'

I nodded and grinned. 'And look after Grandma. So today you can help Grandma collect the eggs and check on the chooks, and Grandma will probably want to do some colouring in...'

'I hate colouring in, it's boring.' He pulled a face. 'Why can't we build something instead?'

'Perfect,' I said. It was like he had read my mind. 'Why don't you work on your fort?'

His face lit up and he clapped his hands with delight. Grandma didn't look so enthused.

'Great idea,' I said. 'While you do that I'll pop into town and get a few bits and pieces to help, then I'll come home and we'll do some more building stuff okay?'

'I'll go have my wash then,' Archie cried, wriggling off the bar stool and heading for the bathroom. 'Come on Grandma, you better get ready too.' He paused at the door and turned back to her. 'But I don't mind if you finish your coffee first,' he said sincerely. 'I'll just wait for you.'

I gave him a wink, feeling the love and pride welling up inside me. While he took off to get ready, I turned to my mother.

'I need your help today,' I said.

She swallowed her mouthful and put the cup down, knowing there was more to it. 'I don't know how good I'll be at building a fort,' she said.

'Doesn't matter, it's about keeping him busy so he's not worrying about Gem. And he knows what he's doing with it, he just needs a hand. The main thing is that I need you two to stay together and keep your eyes open, okay?'

She frowned at me and bristled. 'Of course, I have looked after children before, Mark.'

'I know, but this is different and you need to be vigilant. Come with me.'

I led her to the spare room. The curtains were open and her bedcovers were thrown back. I opened the gun safe and showed her the shotgun and rifle in there.

'Last night I caught two young shitheads trying to break in.'

She looked shocked but said nothing, not even scolding me for my language.

'I ran them off and left them in no doubt what would happen if they came back. But even though I had a gun on them, one of them would still have had a go if he had half a chance.'

'Oh my God.' Grandma took a deep breath. 'That doesn't sound good.'

'No. I'll carry on being on guard when I'm home, but I want you to make sure that you're always handy to a gun. Remember firing the shotgun last year?'

She gave a nervous laugh. 'I remember the bruise on my shoulder. I didn't like that thing.'

'Then use the twenty-two. It barely kicks, it's quieter, and it's got fifteen rounds in the magazine. Here.'

I took it out and gave her a two-minute refresher on handling it, working the bolt and using the safety. I didn't need her to be a marksman; I just needed her to be able to point it at a bad guy and make it go bang.

I could tell she wasn't comfortable but that was too bad. I wasn't comfortable leaving them home alone either, but I couldn't see another way just now.

Archie appeared just as I was putting the Ruger back in the safe. He had his PJ pants pulled over his head like a hat and was cracking himself up.

'Look at me, Dad.'

I laughed with him and even Grandma cheered up at the sound of his laughter.

'I can smell my fart,' he giggled. 'And now my head smells like a butt.'

Normally I would have told him off for talking like that in front of his grandmother, but his humour was contagious and it felt good to forget reality for a moment and get carried away by a happy child. I steered him towards his bedroom instead and told him to get dressed double-quick.

I turned back to my mother. The tension in her face had eased slightly after Archie's joking about.

'It'll be okay,' I said. 'He'll look after you.'

She nodded and gave a wistful smile. 'He's quite a character.'

'He is that.'

'Have you heard from the McMasters'?' she asked abruptly.

'No, I've checked but messages don't seem to be coming through. I don't know what's going on. Maybe there's roadblocks or something.' The *or something* could be a whole raft of things that didn't bear thinking about; looters, a road crash, a breakdown, a medical emergency, who knew? 'We'll just have to wait and see, I guess.'

I started to turn away. She never asked about Gemma's parents in a positive way, so it was yet another conversation to cut short.

'I wish your father was here.'

I stopped in my tracks, unsure if I'd heard right.

My father had walked out years ago, taken up with a younger woman with even younger kids, and it tore the family apart. Understandably there had been a lot of bitterness and resentment but my mother was a master game-player and had always tried to keep her ex-husband within reach. Maintaining a connection with him pulled the other bird's strings too, and Mum had obviously decided that the best way of getting some payback was to mindfuck them both when she could.

I'd never heard her say she missed him though, until now. Maybe it had been about more than just playing with them.

I turned to her, unsure of how to respond. My mother was a tough woman, but for the first time in my memory she looked vulnerable and it threw me. She saw my hesitation and the vulnerability evaporated as fast as it had appeared.

'You better get going if you want to go,' she said abruptly, putting a hand on the door. 'I'll get myself dressed so the little man's not waiting.'

That was my cue and I took it, closing the door between us again.

29

E llerslie was an upper-middle-class city suburb, sandwiched between the wealth of Remuera and the middle/working-class Mount Wellington.

Gemma had flatted there at one point years ago so had some idea of the layout, and she used this to put distance between themselves and the thugs in the V8. Her head was pounding and her legs felt like jelly but she pushed herself on until she felt like throwing up.

By the time she pulled up short in a side street she could no longer hear the roar of the V8 behind them and she guessed they must have covered at least a couple of kilometres. The Ellerslie Racing Club was behind them and over to their left somewhere and they were in a quiet residential street.

She leaned forward with her hands on her knees, her breath tearing at her throat as she fought for oxygen. Sweat soaked her top and ran freely down her face and neck. She spat and sucked down another breath, resisting the urge to throw up. The rock wall at her back was lumpy and covered in ivy. Glancing sideways, she saw Alex finally catch up.

He collapsed on the footpath beside her, sprawling down in a sweaty heap before he started to wretch. He rolled onto his hands and knees and vomited on the path, his body convulsing as he heaved his guts out.

Gemma left him to it and focussed on getting herself under control, finally managing to stand up and draw a full breath. She hadn't realised how unfit she'd become. It hadn't been a long distance they'd covered, but the pressure of the situation added a level of stress she'd never experienced before.

The terror she had felt while the guys in the Holden V8 had screamed around the area, hunting them down, had been unreal. There had been nothing for it but to just run like hell and get out of there. She'd lost count of how many fences she'd climbed, how many properties she'd run through. At one stage a big Alsatian had come racing after them but her fear gave her wings that left the dog for dust.

She shrugged off her daypack and got some water down her, letting some run down her throat and chest. She put the empty bottle back into the pack and looked down, realising she had carried the red first aid kit the whole way. For some reason she hadn't even considered ditching the extra weight.

'Oh Jesus,' Alex moaned. He rolled into a sitting position and leaned back against the rock wall, wiping his mouth on his sleeve. 'Oh my God...'

'You should drink some water,' Gemma said. She watched him struggle to his feet and straighten up. His sweaty face was a picture of pain, and she guessed he was as unfit as she was. Probably worse.

Right now it seemed to be all that he could do to remain upright, without the added pressure of rehydrating.

'Have they gone?' he wheezed.

'I think so.' Gemma looked over her shoulder. 'For now, anyway.' She paused, collecting her thoughts. 'I think I shot one of them.'

'Uh-huh.' Alex fumbled with the zip on his daypack. 'I think you did.' He stopped what he was doing and looked up at her, as if the realisation had just hit him. 'You shot that guy.'

'Yeah.' Gemma nodded, hearing his voice but not seeing him. 'I think I did.' She felt a flutter in her stomach and had the horrible sensation that she was about to throw up. People always did that in the movies, normal people anyway, when they had to kill someone. In a moment the feeling was gone, replaced by a hollow feeling. 'I had to. He was going to shoot me.' She frowned. 'They all were, they were going to kill us. They killed those cops.'

'Uh-huh.' Alex was watching her, waiting to see how she was going to react as she processed the facts. 'I think they would've.'

Gemma stood for a moment, the thoughts tumbling over and over in her head. *I just shot a guy. He was going to kill us.*

This was Mark's world, not hers. Things like this didn't happen to normal people. She was used to working in an office with normal people, talking to normal people about normal things, doing the shopping and the cooking and the cleaning and looking after their house and their son.

Mark's world had some of that too, but it also had a large volume of bad people doing bad things, extreme violence and sadism, the kind of horrible stuff that gave good people nightmares. She wondered how he would have dealt with the guys at the car. She was pretty sure they wouldn't have walked away from it.

But, right now, that didn't matter. Right now, she was alive because she had reacted to a situation that was forced upon her, and she had to be happy with that. She thanked her lucky stars that she had reacted how she did. Fortunately she had at least a basic level of experience with firearms, and the mindset to go with it. She knew it wasn't about being the best with a gun or the hardest or toughest fighter. It was about taking decisive action and not giving up.

With that in mind, she crouched over her daypack and took out the Glock. She found the magazine release button on the left of the grip and dropped out the empty mag. She pulled back on the slide at the top and let it run forward. The other two mags she had grabbed from the gun safe appeared to be full. She loaded one into the butt of the pistol, hearing it click into place and remembering to slap the baseplate to make sure it was seated; Mark always did that with his .22 rifle.

She pulled the slide back and let it go forward again, knowing this would put a bullet in the chamber so the gun was good to go. She took a few moments checking for a safety catch before remembering Mark had said the Glock didn't have one. 'Your trigger finger is your safety,' he'd told her once.

Gemma put the empty magazine into her daypack, removed the spare from its pouch and slipped it into her pocket, and zipped up the bag again. She stood and carefully secured the pistol in the front of her waistband, where she could easily grab it. She realised that Alex was watching her.

'What?' she said.

'I dunno,' he said, 'it's just...you look kind of...comfortable with that. Like you know what you're doing.'

Gemma felt her eyebrows raise at his description. 'I don't know if *comfortable* is the right word,' she said. 'And I never thought I'd be running around with a gun, that's for sure. But it's a better alternative than being raped or shot.'

He gave her a doubtful look. 'I don't know about getting raped...' he said.

'Well you probably don't need to, do you?' she retorted, with more heat than she'd intended. 'But I don't think those guys were out collecting for the Red Cross, were they?'

'It's a bit of a stretch,' he persisted, forcing himself to his feet.

'Think what you like, Alex,' Gemma told him bluntly. 'But I'm not going to let some arsehole like that get their hands on me. If Mark had been there he would have killed every single one of them and not even batted an eye.'

Alex studied her dubiously. She could almost see the cogs churning in his head. *What the hell have I got myself into here? She's crazy.*

'He sounds like a hard man,' he said.

Gemma pondered that for a second before giving her head a short shake. 'Tough,' she said, 'but not hard.'

'Same thing isn't it?'

'Hard means you have no feelings. Tough means you're strong but still have feelings.' She hitched the daypack on her shoulders. 'Mark has feelings. You just don't want to cross him, that's all.'

Alex slung his own bag onto his back, then picked up the red first aid pack. 'I guess I better carry this since you've got the gun,' he said. 'I don't want to get shot for arguing with you, Gemma.'

She frowned and was about to snap at him when she caught the teasing look on his face. 'Ha ha, very funny. Just don't drop it because you're so tired,' she said.

She looked around, getting her bearings. There was no traffic on the road and no birdsong in the trees. She could hear vehicles further away, the rumble of a truck, the roar of a chainsaw – who the hell was chain sawing today? she wondered – and a helicopter somewhere in the distance. Nobody had come out of their house since they'd been there, but she guessed people were probably there, hidden away inside.

'We need to keep heading south,' she said, thinking aloud. 'It'd be great if we could get our hands on a car. Or even bikes. If we keep on walking then we might come across something that'll speed us up.'

'How long do you think it'll take us to get to Manukau?' Alex asked.

Gemma shrugged. 'I don't know. Hopefully we should get there today, but it depends what we come across I guess. The sooner we get going, the better.'

30

The biggest bonus of travelling in a motorhome was being fully self-contained.

The McMasters had spent a comfortable night in a double bed, warm and secure, disturbed only by the movements and noise of fellow stranded travellers. They woke early to the sounds of arguing nearby and listened to a couple venting their frustrations at each other. Apparently he was a moron for not gassing the car up before they left and she was a selfish bitch for hogging the only blanket all night.

Sandy prepared a breakfast of cereal and canned fruit with milk from the chilly bin, and boiled the jug on the gas stove for a strong cup of tea. Rob dressed himself and went outside, surveying their surroundings again. Nothing appeared to have changed overnight aside from the couple glaring at each other beside the lowered and tinted Toyota rocket in the next lane.

They were in their mid-twenties – millennials, he thought they were called these days – and looked dishevelled and grumpy. He had pants down around his arse and a skater hoody. She wore tight jeans and her hair was bleached within an inch of its life.

Rob gave them a nod and the girl nodded back. The guy looked sullen and ignored him.

'Rough night?' Rob said.

The girl nodded again and he could see she was on the verge of tears. The guy scowled to show how fierce he was.

'Have you got any food?' Rob said.

They gave each other daggers and the girl wiped her nose. 'No,' she said.

'I s'pose you've got a kitchen in there,' the guy sneered, 'in your fancy fuckin' house bus.'

Rob looked at him coolly, letting his gaze settle on the guy's face until the younger man looked away and scowled some more.

'We do have a kitchen,' he said, 'and there's no call for that kind of attitude. It's been a crappy night for you by the looks of it, and I was going to offer you a cup of tea. But if you don't want it...'

'Yes please,' the girl said quickly, giving her boyfriend another look. 'We'd love one.'

The guy started to sneer again but the girl cut him off. 'Don't be a dick, Josh,' she said. 'He's being nice.' She turned back to Rob. 'Sorry,' she said.

Rob nodded. 'Sugar?'

'Two please.'

He returned shortly with two steaming paper cups and handed them over. The girl took hers gratefully and the guy even muttered a surly thank you. Rob stepped back so as not to crowd them, noticing that other people were milling around by their vehicles as well, idling chatting or just standing.

Waiting. Everybody waiting for help that wasn't going to come.

The smell of petrol was still strong in the air and he wondered how long it would take for someone to light up a smoke. Hopefully back here it wouldn't pose a risk but closer to the crash scene it would be catastrophic. Igniting the fumes would cause a chain reaction of fires and explosions down the highway of packed cars and dozens of people would be killed and injured.

Rob felt his gut tighten as the realisation hit him. They needed to get the hell out of here.

Sandy came up beside him, her hands tucked into the pockets of her windproof jacket. She smiled at the young couple, who were now well into their cups of tea and seeming to brighten up, even the guy.

'Is anything moving?' she asked.

'Not yet,' Rob said. 'But it needs to. All these cars need to get going, but we need help to do it.'

'And I take it you have a plan?' Sandy's eyes twinkled behind her glasses – she knew her husband well.

Rob gave a small smile and outlined his plan to her. Sandy nodded her approval. As the young couple were finishing their drinks, Rob introduced himself and shook hands.

Josh and Sienna were soon listening to his plan and nodding their agreement. Rob set them on their tasks and made his way to the cars behind the motorhome. As soon as he started talking to the motorists there, people began to drift over to listen, and within a few minutes the crowd was growing bigger and more people were sifting down the line to spread the word.

Sandy stayed behind the wheel in the bus for two important reasons – they wanted to be ready to move as soon as possible, and Rob was conscious that such a vehicle was an obvious target for thieves, either to steal outright or to loot for provisions. Sandy kept the doors and windows locked and the key in the ignition, ready to go.

By the time Rob had walked a few hundred metres down the highway, he could see the tailback snaking back past the side road. The fact that people had elected to sit on the highway all night in their cars, rather than taking a side road and trying to get out, astounded him. Perhaps they were too reliant on GPS and didn't have the gumption to have a go. Perhaps they were just sheep that followed the sheep in front of them.

Whatever the reason, a lot of these people had made their own situation worse. As usual it took someone like him to come along and fix it for them. Rob sighed inwardly. If it took holding their hand to make his own situation better then that was what he would do.

Josh and Sienna were coming back towards him, having walked down to the side road and started spreading the word from down there. In the distance, Rob could see vehicles starting to move as people got themselves going.

He walked with them back towards their own vehicles. As they walked, Josh fell into step beside him.

'Sorry for being a dick,' he said quietly.

Rob chuckled. 'Don't worry mate, we're all dicks at times.'

'Thanks for helping us out.'

Rob nodded. 'No worries, I'm sure you'd do the same for someone else.' He glanced sideways at the younger man. 'Have you run out of gas?'

'That's the other thing I was going to ask.' Josh looked sheepish. 'I don't s'pose you've got any spare gas have you?'

'Got a little bit. How far are you going?'

'Raglan.'

Rob whistled. Raglan was a small town on the west coast of the Waikato, a couple of hours' drive from where they were now. That was a fair hike in the current circumstances and they had a lot of highway driving to get there.

'Let's see what we've got, eh?'

Even though they hadn't picked up as much gas as he would've liked, Rob felt for the younger couple and didn't want to see them stranded on the side of the road again. With things the way they were just now, anything could happen. Sienna was a pretty young thing and he doubted either her or Josh had the skills or mindset to protect themselves.

He poured about ten litres from a spare fuel can into their tank and recapped the container.

'Should be enough to get you to Pokeno or Mercer,' he said. 'Hopefully you can get more at the gas station there. Or the pumps at Hampton Downs or down in Te Kauwhata.'

'Thanks,' Josh said, closing his fuel cap. 'Appreciate it.'

'Thank you so much.' Sienna gave him a hug and waved to Sandy, who had buzzed down the window.

'Looks like we're moving,' Rob said, seeing the queue behind them starting to inch back. 'Good luck.'

Sandy moved across to the passenger seat and he climbed up behind the wheel. It still took another half hour before they actually got to move, but just the anticipation of it lifted their spirits. When it came to their turn, Rob let Josh turn around and head in the right direction before following suit. The motorhome was nearly as manoeuvrable as a car but it didn't stop someone from honking their horn for him to hurry up.

'Jerk,' Sandy muttered.

Rob ignored the other driver and focussed on getting around and into the correct lane. Already somebody had had a nose to tail up ahead and two cars were stopped while the drivers remonstrated with each other.

'More jerks,' Sandy commented. 'Seems to be a morning for them.'

Rob felt himself smile. 'You're a box of birds this morning,' he said.

Sandy peered over her glasses at him. 'The sooner we get there the better. I'm all for camping in the van, but this is not what I had in mind.'

31

W hen I got to the Pukekohe Police Station I found the car
park full and more cars double parked outside on the
road, some on the footpath.

The crowd at the front entrance was so big it was spilling outside.
There were more people down the side of the building at the vehicle
gate, and I could see a couple of uniforms on the inside of the gate.
Whether they were talking or not I had no idea; it was hard to hear
over the shouting of the crowd at the front.

The station was a single storey white concrete block with a small
glass-walled front foyer and a narrow garden out the front. On one
side was a car dealership and on the other were a couple of small
businesses. The windows of the station were all covered internally by
blinds so it was hard to tell if anyone was inside.

What had always been a normal, friendly local station now
resembled a place under siege. I had avoided the highway patrol base
at Pokeno and the four-man station at Tuakau to come here, because
it was the area HQ. I hadn't made the decision for a third trip to
Pukekohe lightly, but I needed information.

I dropped the truck across the road outside a lawnmower shop and trotted over. There was plenty of traffic around and nobody seemed too bothered about pedestrian safety. I went down the side driveway past the first crowd and angled towards a side door that I knew was regularly used. I knocked on it and looked towards the nearest window, seeing the blind twitch after my second knock.

A moment later the door opened and a middle-aged uniformed cop told me to hurry up and get inside. I did as I was told before the crowd realised there was another way in and he shut the door behind me.

The guy looked at me and I recognised his face but had to check his name badge.

'Gidday Steve,' I said, as if we were old friends. 'Looks a bit busy out there, mate.'

'Oh fuck, you've got no idea.' The stress was pounding off him. 'These people want answers we can't give them, they want help we can't fuckin' give them, and there's no bastard in charge here.' He ran a hand through his greying hair. 'It's all fucked mate, and all I wanna do is get home to Donna and the kids, but of course I can't.'

'Where're all the bosses?'

'Crisis meeting up at Manukau, trying to sort out what the hell we're gunna do. In the meantime all the patrols are out and we've only got a skeleton staff here.'

I heard a booming voice from the direction of the front counter. It was a voice I knew.

'What's that fuckwit doing here?' I said.

Steve rolled his eyes. 'Lives in Patumahoe, doesn't he? Thought he'd be better off down here for a while, he even took over someone else's office.'

The voice belonged to Superintendent Artie Darroch, AKA the Artful Dodger. He'd barely done a day's policing in his life but rose through the ranks via support groups where he didn't need any actual policing skills. He'd bullied and harassed so many people along the way that nobody wanted to work with him, and he'd ended up being given a made-up job at the district HQ at Manukau just to keep him out of the way.

He was also the man in charge of my case and had taken great pleasure in making the whole experience as difficult as possible for me.

'I'm ordering you all to leave the station immediately,' he was shouting. 'If you don't leave on your own, you will be made to leave. Now go!'

The people at the counter were clamouring for attention, shouting over each other, each voice adding to the level of tension and energy in the crowd. Even without seeing them I could tell this wasn't going to end well.

'I don't know who he thinks is going to force them out,' Steve muttered. 'There's only me and three others here, plus the two ladies at the front.' He looked at me. 'What're you here for anyway?'

'Information,' I said. 'There's fuck-all coming over the radio and I want to know what's actually going on.'

Steve shook his head gravely. 'It's not good,' he said.

'No shit.'

He jerked a thumb in the direction of the front counter. 'No point asking that arsehole for any info.' He frowned as a thought struck him. 'Not wanting to be funny, but are you even allowed to be here? In a police station?'

I shrugged. 'As far as I know.'

'What the hell is he doing here?' bellowed a voice from up the hallway. We both turned to see Darroch poking his head around the doorway from the front counter area. He looked surprisingly unhappy to see me.

'Pretty much the same as the rest of the civilians here, Dodger,' I said, deliberately using the nickname he hated.

'Get him the hell out of my station!' Darroch shouted at Steve, before ducking back out of view again. The raised voices continued out the front and Steve shrugged apologetically.

'So it's his station now, I guess,' he said with a tight grin.

'Fuck 'im,' I said. 'He couldn't...'

I was interrupted by shouting, Darroch and several other voices all going for it, accompanied by a female's shriek.

'Back off or I'll shoot! I'll shoot you! Armed Police!' Darroch screeched.

Steve and I both bolted for the front counter, and Steve raced through the doorway into the office area where Darroch and the two Watchouse ladies stood on our side of the counter. A couple of people were up on the counter itself, trying to clamber over the security wires there, and Darroch had a Glock trained on them. He was still screeching at them and they were still ignoring him. God only knew what he was doing with a gun but it was a terrible idea to have presented it right now.

A couple more people reached across the counter and somebody grabbed one of the Watchouse ladies, Bev, by the arm and pulled her forward until she was half on top of the counter. Whoever that was started whaling on her and Steve leaped to her aid.

Somebody in the crowd threw a bottle and it hit the wall near Darroch's head, exploding fizzy drink everywhere.

The Glock went off and one of the people trying to get over the wire barrier yelped and fell backwards as if they were crowd surfing. In all the confusion I couldn't even tell if it was a male or a female.

The crowd started to stampede, some going for the doors, others just crashing into each other. People were falling and getting trampled and in seconds someone had crashed through the glass exit doors, scattering glass everywhere.

I stayed back out of the way, not wanting to be anywhere near Darroch and his shooter. It seemed that I had probably overstayed my welcome anyway, but there was no way I wanted to exit out the front with that crowd there.

Steve had freed Bev from her attacker and was now trying to console her and her colleague, both of them crying and distressed. Darroch turned to me and I could see his eyes were out on stalks.

'What're you doing here?' he shouted. 'Get out! Get out now!'

'Probably not your best decision,' I remarked, not moving.

'You saw them, they were savages! They were going to kill us!'

That was a bit of a stretch from what I had seen, but I figured it was best not to argue with an idiot with a gun. I could see that the crowd had all gone now but I could still hear them out the front, shouting and screaming.

Darroch turned on Steve, bellowing at him to secure the front doors. Steve left the women to do so and Darroch turned back to me.

'What's the rest of the plan?' I asked.

He glared at me. 'It doesn't concern you what the plan is,' he snapped. 'You're a civilian now, so you can just get out of the station. This is a restricted area anyway.'

He came towards me with the Glock in his hand. It was pointed towards the ground but I had seen how quickly he'd overreacted before, so I backed up.

'You've got a big problem on your hands here mate,' I told him. 'Those people won't stay away, whether you've got guns or not. If they want to get in here, they will.'

'Not while I'm in command,' Darroch replied, sounding like a B-movie actor. 'Now move.'

'Kind of ironic,' I said, turning towards the side door I had entered earlier. 'You shoot someone for climbing on the counter, and I'm the one who gets the boot for excessive force.'

Darroch gave a snort. 'Shut up and get out,' he said, jabbing a finger at the door. 'You're nothing but a thug. You were a disgrace to the uniform right from the start.'

My blood was boiling and I wanted nothing more than to wring his neck, but I kept myself in check. I didn't care about proving him right or wrong, but I was certain that he would just shoot me if I attacked him.

I put a hand on the door handle and paused. I could hear the crowd outside but they didn't sound too close. Maybe I could slip away without being noticed.

'Move it or I'll arrest you,' Darroch snapped.

I pushed through the door. It was probably time to get home anyway. Hopefully the McMasters' had arrived by now. It was obvious that I wasn't going to get the information I sought.

Emerging out into the air, all hope of slipping away disappeared immediately. The crowd had grown in numbers so there were maybe fifty or so people gathered in the driveway, a few of them tending to someone on the ground. I could see now that it was a man and he was bleeding from a wound to the shoulder.

The scariest thing about this crowd was that most of them were just normal people. A few shitkickers were amongst them for good measure, but by far most of them could have been my neighbours or members of my family. It didn't bode well.

The crowd were riled up already, and the sight of me emerging was enough to spur a few into more shouting. The door banged shut behind me and I saw some of the bolder ones start to come forward. They were several metres away but their intent was pretty clear.

'He's one of them,' somebody called out, 'I saw him in there.'

'Fuckin' arsehole,' somebody else shouted. 'We only come to ask for help.'

'Same here,' I replied, 'they kicked me out too.'

Any hope of solidarity from these guys disappeared the moment I laid eyes on Stew Patten. He was a self-appointed community activist, the sort of dickhead that turned up to every protest or rally going, who wrote a constant stream of letters to the local paper, and who complained about every interaction with cops that he'd had in his miserable life. He was a scrawny little no-chest prick but he was vocal and a section of the community saw him as the little guy standing up against The Man.

'He's a cop,' Patten called out, his eyes locked on mine. 'I know him.'

He certainly did. I'd once dragged him out of a protest against a visiting dignitary up in the city, managing to ruffle his thinning hair in the process, and spent the next two years being investigated for it.

I shook my head and began to head past them, moving with purpose to dissuade any of them.

A few more insults were thrown my way and I continued walking, nearly past them when Patten spoke up again.

'He's one of them that shot Richie.'

That was the final straw for the hotheads amongst them, and I was grabbed from behind as I broke into a run. I tried to pull free but there were several of them and someone got an arm around my throat, bending me over backwards and throwing me to the ground.

They piled in on top and I was taking punches and kicks all over. All I could do was curl up and cover my head, hoping the cops would intervene before these pricks killed me.

I took a decent boot to the back and someone began stomping my ribs and hip. I tried to roll away but got a boot in the guts for my efforts. I didn't hear any shouts other than the guys above me hurling insults and egging each other on, but finally the stench of pepper spray reached my nostrils. I recognised it immediately and screwed my eyes shut, trying to hold my breath.

The kicking and stomping stopped and I heard more cursing, accompanied by the odd thump of a baton against a body.

I stayed where I was until hands rolled me over and I heard Steve's voice.

'Get up, get up. You're okay.'

My body was telling me otherwise but I let him help me up anyway. The crowd had broken up but was still there, a few on the ground either taken out by OC spray or the batons wielded by Steve and his uniformed colleagues, and I got the feeling this was just a temporary reprieve.

Darroch appeared now that the action was over, and began directing the cops to arrest some of the stragglers that were close to hand. I didn't see the point myself; surely he wanted them to clear off rather than hang around? Then his gaze fell on me.

'And him,' he called out, pointing at me.

Steve looked back at him. 'Are you sure?'

Darroch's face darkened. 'Don't question me, Constable! Arrest that man and get him inside with the others.'

It crossed my mind that I should just run for it, knowing Steve wouldn't put up much of a chase, but I could see that Darroch still had the Glock in his hand. I didn't trust the bastard not to shoot me in the back.

I decided I better roll with it for now and see what happened, but with one eye out for the first opportunity to get the hell out of there. Steve looked apologetic and I shrugged my shoulders; *what can you do?* To be fair to him, he never actually told me I was under arrest, but I followed him anyway.

32

The others were all struggling with the cops and some of their mates tried to join in, which only filled the air with more pepper spray and sent them reeling back, coughing and spluttering.

I was pleased to see that Stew Patten was one of them that had been grabbed.

We made our way through the vehicle gate and round the back of the station, where there was a drive-in cage that accessed the old cell block. The cells were no longer officially in use, with all prisoners supposed to be transported up to the district HQ at Manukau, but down here in Pukekoke they did things their way.

The door was opened and we were ushered into a cold concrete corridor with cells branching off it. This was an old-school cell block with barred doors and big keys, no fancy cameras or electronic locking systems.

Besides me there were six other prisoners, including two women. One of the guys was a pie addict with a bushy beard, another was about my size and fitter looking, the third was a skinnier guy with a mullet hairdo and a Led Zeppelin T shirt, and then there was Stew Patten. The two women were put in a cell across the corridor from us and the four men and I were shown into a larger holding cell. It had steel bench seats around the walls, all marked with graffiti.

From the way the Led Zeppelin guy moved away from the others and sat by himself, I guessed he wasn't part of their group. The other three stood together, huddled in a corner and talking in hushed tones.

The door was clanged shut and Steve looked through the bars, catching my eye.

'I'll try and find out what's going on,' he said quietly and I nodded my thanks. I had no desire to be there any longer than I needed to be, particularly with these numbskulls.

He followed his colleagues up the corridor, a barrage of abuse from the two women echoing off the walls behind him, and I turned away from the door.

Led Zep was sitting on a bench seat with his arms folded, looking mighty pissed off. I sat along from him, choosing to keep my own counsel for now. With any luck we'd be out of there shortly.

'So are you a cop?' Led Zep said.

'Na,' I said. 'I used to be, not anymore. Long time ago.' It wasn't long at all, but he didn't need to know that.

'So how come you're in here?' he persisted. 'Weren't you the one who got his ass kicked out there?'

'I am.' I nodded, keeping the other three in my peripheral vision. 'And I'm here because the boss out there doesn't like me.'

He gave me a curious look.

'He's a fuckwit,' I said. I couldn't think of a better explanation.

'Fuck.' Led Zep let out a sigh. 'I only came down here to find out what the hell's going on. They're not saying much on the radio and we lost our power at home. The supermarket's got fuck-all food unless you want Chinese noodles three times a day.'

'It's not good,' I agreed.

I saw the little group begin to move and looked up to see they were fanning out in front of us. Patten was at the end and slightly back, like the brave leader he was. The fit guy was right in front of me. He was about thirty and unshaven, with a crewcut and a few tats on his bare arms. He was clearly the muscle in the crew, and it didn't surprise me. So-called passive activists like Patten had always been backed up by thugs who were there for the fight, not the cause.

'So you shot our friend Richie,' the thug said, flexing his fingers.

'No,' I said evenly, 'that was the Superintendent out there. You know, the one with the gun?'

'We all saw you do it,' he said, gesturing towards his two mates. Patten had a sly smirk on his face, knowing full well what was about to happen. The fat guy was huffing and puffing and already looked flushed. 'So now we'll even the score, one to one. Man to man.' He eyeballed me. 'Unless you're only brave when you're hiding behind your badge?'

I suppressed the urge to roll my eyes. I'd had about enough of this, but now was not the time to get into a debate. And there was as much chance of this being a one on one as there was of the fat guy running a hundred metres.

The options weren't looking great and I mentally willed Steve to hurry up and get back here. I was about to speak when the smell of smoke hit me. I shot a look across the corridor and could see smoke in the cell opposite. The two women were standing over a crappy thin mattress that had been on the bunk in their cell, and the mattress was smoking. Like us, they obviously hadn't been searched, and I knew from experience that a fire in a cell block would only take a few minutes to be a huge problem.

'Tell them to put that bloody fire out,' I snapped at Patten. 'The smoke'll kill us all.'

He shrugged and smirked a bit more, so I turned my attention to them instead, telling them the same thing.

'Fuck you, arsehole,' one of them shouted back at me, already coughing from the fumes. 'They'll have to let us out.'

I was about to respond when I caught a flash of movement from the corner of my eye. The thug had obviously lost patience and decided a blind shot was a good idea to get the ball rolling. I raised my arm just in time to avoid a broken cheekbone, but the punch was hard enough to knock me sideways on the bench seat. I went with it, scrambling away from him until I could get to my feet. Exposing my back allowed him to land a couple of good hits but I got up, pushed off the wall and spun with my arms up, blocking another swing.

The thug was in close, determined to cause some damage, and he seemed to have some skills.

The problem with guys like that is that they're used to hitting either a punching bag or someone smaller than them, or their girl-friend. They're not used to guys that are prepared to fight back and have few boundaries, and that was the category I fell squarely into.

I took the next hit on my forearms and pushed forward, not giving him room for another shot. As he started to back pedal, I landed a solid left jab to the side of his head and followed it with a right jab to his gut. He took them, kept his feet and danced away from me.

I was shoved from behind and went off balance, allowing him to step in with a good hook to my jaw. I stumbled, hit the wall and took a follow up hook to the other side of my head. Lights popped and for a second I nearly went down, until he came in again and threw a shot at my face. He was over confident from his previous hits and the punch was loose.

I ducked, pushed off and grabbed him round the waist, driving him back across the cell. He slammed into the wall opposite with a loud explosion of air from his lungs. I pulled back and went for gold, throwing fists and elbows at his face and head as fast as I could.

He took several hits and started to slump, and I would have dropped him quickly if the fat guy hadn't had other ideas. He crashed into me from behind, body slamming me into the thug who hit the wall again and went down.

The fat guy was throwing punches at me now but he was too close to get any power into them. I wriggled away, shoving him off me and turning, ready to face the new threat. That was when Patten got me with a cheap shot, a kick to the back which threw me forward into the fat guy.

The smoke was stinging my eyes and the air was pretty acrid already, which coupled with my panting and the fat guy squeezing me, made it pretty hard to breathe. I could hear Led Zep shouting for help somewhere in the background, and the two women were going to town too.

The fat guy started trying to bite my ear as if he was a South African rugby player and I shook my head to try and get away. *Fuck it, enough was enough.*

I threw knees and hands at him until I got free and I stepped back, slapping away his grabbing hands. I lined him up and landed a right jab straight on his nose, spraying blood and giving it an audible crunch as the bone snapped. He fell back against the wall, grabbing at his face and wailing, all the fight gone out of him.

I spun, catching Patten sneaking up behind me again, and I gave him a hard shove in the chest that sent him back into the wall. I was turning back to the other two when the cops arrived, fighting through the smoke that was clouding the air. They went to the women's cell first, throwing the door open and unleashing an extinguisher with a huge cloud of white powder that clogged the air even more.

The thug was picking himself up off the floor and I could see blood on his face. As he came up he brought a knife out of his pocket, a cheap plastic box cutter that probably cost him five bucks at a hardware store. He thumbed the blade out until a couple of inches was showing and steadied himself.

'Give us a hand here!' I shouted to the cops. 'He's got a knife!'

The thug lunged forward and I stepped back and to the side, slapping his hand away and continuing to move, trying to get behind him. He slashed at me with no technique, just big swings that would open me up if any of them connected. I jumped back, stumbled over the fat guy's legs and cracked my head against the concrete wall as I landed sideways on the bench seat.

Led Zep had scrambled away into the corner, trying to stay out of the way, too scared to intervene. Patten was dancing away, staying in the background, and the fat guy was still down, spitting out strings of blood.

'I'm gunna cut you up you fuckin' faggot,' the thug panted, slashing again. I pulled back but felt the blade nick my cheek as it swished past.

I got both hands up, just missing his wrist, and instead I kicked out. I booted him hard in the ribs, knocking him backwards, and I lunged up to catch him while he was off balance. He slashed again but I was ready this time, and I caught his wrist as the knife went by. I locked onto his wrist and hand, wrenching and twisting hard so his hand bent like a gooseneck. He squealed but wouldn't release the knife, and he kicked at my shins.

Patten came in and gave me another sneaky punch in the back, distracting me just enough for the thug to get some leverage back in his hand. Patten gave me another hit and I knew that if he came into the game properly then I would probably lose.

The thug was twisting, trying to get free, and he threw an awkward left overhand at me. I ducked aside, missed it, and came back up with a straight-knuckle strike aimed at his throat. Unfortunately for him he was starting to come forward at the same time, bringing extra force to the impact as my knuckles slammed into his Adam's apple.

He gasped and dropped everything, clutching for his throat with his eyes bugging out, and he went down in a sitting position on the floor. I left him to it and spun on my heels, seeing Patten backing away with his hands up defensively.

The clang of the door keys behind us was the only thing that saved him. Led Zep bolted out of the cell and somebody grabbed me, pulling me out after him. The corridor was filled with smoke and extinguisher powder and I could hardly see a thing. The two women were coughing their lungs out by the exit door, where a cop was wrestling with the key.

'There's three guys still in there!' I shouted, my eyes stinging from the smoke.

The cop who'd grabbed me ducked into the holding cell and I went after him, grabbing the fat guy by an arm and helping him up. He was mumbling and spitting blood but got to his feet, and I pushed him out into the corridor. I felt people bumping against me as we headed for the light of the open door.

Patten was hustled out by the cop and, even though he was being saved, he still had the cheek to tell the cop to get his hands off him. The cop shoved him up against the wall and told him to shut his mouth and get moving. I grinned to myself and stood aside to let the activist get past.

'There's another guy in there,' I said to the cop, my throat raspy.

He shook his head. 'He's dead,' he said.

I felt my guts drop to the floor. That was a game changer, right there.

We got out into the fresh air of the yard, and I saw the two women huddling around a hose, washing their faces and hacking like a pair of lifelong smokers. I wondered if the crazy bitches knew they had nearly killed us all. Right now I had bigger things to worry about, and Patten wasn't about to let me forget it.

'He killed my friend,' he was snarling at Darroch, pointing at me. 'He beat my friend to death in there and I saw the whole thing.'

Darroch had donned a stab vest now and had his Glock holstered on his hip. Standing with him were Steve and the cop who'd pulled me out. He turned and looked at me.

'Is that so?' he said. 'Constable, is that true?'

The cop remained non-committal. 'There is a guy in there and he's dead,' he said. 'I've closed the cell door to preserve the scene. I don't know how he died, though. Maybe smoke inhalation.'

Patten nutted off then, yelling and waving his arms around. The fat guy roused himself enough to give his two cents' worth as well, although he was difficult to understand with a broken nose.

Led Zep was standing to the side saying nothing, and I caught his eye. 'What do you reckon mate?' I said. 'You saw the three of them attack me in there, you saw that guy with a knife. Here.' I showed the cut on my cheek to the cops. 'He cut me there.'

Darroch looked to Led Zep, who had no desire to get involved at all. Eventually Led Zep gave a bit of a shrug. 'They did attack him,' he said. 'Mostly the guy in there and this guy.' He indicated the fat man.

'Sounds like self-defence to me then,' Steve piped up, and Darroch gave him a withering look.

'Get him inside, I'll come and deal with him in a minute.'

Steve ushered me back inside where the breeze was clearing the corridor. We walked past the holding cell and I paused, seeing the thug lying half slumped against the wall. There was no question that he was dead and I was pretty sure I was responsible. The funny thing was, although I had butterflies in my stomach, I felt no remorse about it. He had tried to kill me and I'd defended myself, nothing more. The fact that he'd died was his own fault; I knew within myself that I'd had no choice. It could just as easily have been me lying there, probably with a knife planted in my hand.

We walked on and Steve took me through to the meal room, a large airy room with a kitchen attached. It was at the back corner of the building and the wide windows gave a good view of the station's car park and up the driveway past the gate.

'You want a drink?' Steve asked, heading towards the kitchen.

I nodded, looking past him out the window. I could see that the crowd from earlier had returned, or maybe they'd just never left, and were gathered at the gate. Steve saw them too and he stopped midstride.

'Oh fuck,' he said. 'Gun!'

33

Steve ducked down before I realised what was happening, and a second later the window above the kitchen sink shattered, accompanied by the crack of a shot. I ducked down and another shot flew through the empty window frame, exploding a framed picture on the wall into a thousand pieces.

I could hear shouts from outside and the rattle of the gate and fence as people started to climb over. Steve crab-walked over to me and we made for the door, hearing another shot blow out more glass behind us.

'What the fuck are they doing?' Steve panted. His eyes were wide and he was on the verge of panicking. I remembered now that he was a Youth Aid officer; his job involved meetings and talking to families and social workers, not dealing with mobs of people who were trying to shoot you.

'They'll be in the station in a minute unless we do something,' I croaked, my throat still scratchy. I'd never got that drink. 'Where's your gun safe?'

'It's empty,' he said. 'They're all in the cars.'

'Which are out.'

'And I think the boss grabbed the last Glock.'

Another shot sounded outside and there was more shouting. Risking a glance around the doorway I saw that Patten, the fat guy and the two women were over at the fence now and there was three or four climbing over. They were stuck at the top due to the single strand of barbed wire, but that wouldn't hold them up for long. I could see one guy with a rifle at his shoulder and another guy further along, loading what looked like a bolt action rifle.

I looked back at Steve. 'What about exhibits?' I said.

Every Police station has an exhibits store of some sort, and in a rural area like this, more often than not it doubled as a store for recovered or surrendered firearms. All of these were supposed to go up to Manukau, but of course Pukekohe did things their way.

'Down here.'

Steve led the way down the internal hallway to the Resource Room, where he grabbed a set of keys off a hook. I wondered where Darroch, Led Zep, the Watchouse ladies and the other cops had got to. Steve unlocked an internal door and it opened up to a small exhibits store with shelves that were full to bursting with items in Kleensaks and plastic bags.

One section of it resembled a wine rack, but instead of bottles the slots contained firearms. I could tell at a glance that most of them were probably crap, but beggars couldn't be choosers.

I started sliding them out, and quickly realised that my assessment had been right.

'Anything decent?' I asked Steve. 'And anything with ammo?'

'Here,' he said, grabbing a wooden box off a separate shelf and handing it to me. 'This was found at a search warrant last week. Couldn't ID an owner.'

I took the box and opened it. Inside was a blued Ruger GP100 .357 Magnum with a four-inch barrel. It had a black leather Bianchi holster and a pair of loaded speed loaders with it. It was a quality weapon. I opened the cylinder and loaded it with one of the speed loaders, shoving the empty with the full one into my pocket.

'Find a couple of shotguns that work,' I said, threading the holster onto my belt.

I was buckling up when Steve handed me an over/under Nikko 12-gauge. It was a skeet gun with probably 28-inch barrels. He fumbled around for some ammo while I checked our backs. I could hear the odd shot coming, the rifles mixed with the lighter pop of a pistol, which I presumed was Darroch with his Glock.

Steve was still bumbling about when the other two cops came running down the hall. I quickly lowered the Ruger when I realised it was them.

'Where are the others?' I asked.

'That fuckin' idiot's out there trading shots with them like it's the fuckin' Alamo,' one of them said, pushing past me to get into the exhibits store. I moved out of the way as they clearly had the same idea as me, and when I emerged into the main office I could hear glass breaking out at the front counter.

'Hurry up Steve,' I called over my shoulder. 'They're coming in the front.'

'We'll sort them out,' the same cop said, pushing past me again.

Both of them drew boxy yellow Tasers from their belts and headed towards the Watchouse as I gave Steve the hurry-up for some ammo. He finally came up with a box of birdshot and I broke open the Nikko to load it. He'd found himself a side by side 12-gauge and a handful of shells and was busy loading it, muttering to himself as he fumbled with the rounds. The twin barrels of his shotgun had been cut down to about 18 inches, but the walnut stock was fully intact.

I heard a great crash from the front followed by shouting and running feet.

'Taser 50,000 volts, stop there! Put it down!'

'Fuck youse!'

'Taser, Taser, Taser!'

There was the boom of a shot in confined quarters, a scream, and all hell broke loose. A Taser zapped and crackled, shouts came, another boom, more screaming, another zap.

I hurried forward, shoving the box of ammo into my back pocket, the Nikko at the ready. Going through the internal door to the hallway that led to the front counter – where I'd been kicked out the side door earlier – I could hear a wet gurgling sound from just round the corner and the crunch of broken glass a few metres away.

Glancing round the doorframe I saw the cop who'd helped me out of the cells, sprawled on his side just inside the Watchouse. His Taser was discarded nearby and the front of his stab vest was turning dark red as blood bubbled out of a hole in his chest. Blood was frothing at his mouth and running down his chin.

The other Taser zapped again from somewhere this side of the front counter, then I saw a guy jump up on the other side and unleash a wild shot from a rifle. It was loud and frightening at such close range, and the guy was yelling like a madman.

As I was turning away he dropped back out of sight, and at the same time someone else booted in the door that led from the front foyer into the hallway just a few metres in front of me. The door crashed open, splinters of wood flying, and the handle flew off. A guy in a red and black checked Swandri stepped across the threshold, a machete in his hand. I brought the Nikko up and presented it at him.

'Get back!' Staring at the wrong end of a double-barrelled shotgun is not a good place to be, but this guy didn't bat an eyelid. Either he was retarded or he was on meth, or maybe both.

'Agghhhh!' He raised the machete and charged at me.

I squeezed the trigger and the shotgun kicked hard against my shoulder. The shot was deafening and the pellets took him in the gut, knocking him flat on his back in the doorway. The guy with the rifle appeared behind him, peering round the doorframe, and I unleashed the second barrel at him. He disappeared from sight and I ruined the paintwork of the foyer wall instead. Scrambling backwards and drawing the Ruger at the same time, I bumped into Steve and knocked him into the wall.

'Watch out,' he mumbled, looking at me rather than the open doorway beyond us.

The guy with the rifle appeared again and I shoved Steve aside, getting the Ruger up and squeezing off a shot. The rifle boomed a nano-second later and a round punched into the wall beside Steve. He jumped with fright and squeezed the first trigger of his shotgun, blasting a hole in the ceiling. Plaster dust showered us as we got back round the corner out of sight.

'Sorry,' Steve was muttering, 'sorry, sorry. Oh fuck, sorry, sorry.'

He was clearly going into shock and I doubted he'd be of any use to me. I handed the Nikko off to Steve and took the sawn-off from him. It was a Webley and Scott with a walnut stock and tarnished metal work. It would be much easier to wield in confined spaces than the Nikko. I quickly broke it open, reloaded, and snapped it shut again. Keeping an eye on the hallway, I handed the box of ammo to Steve and re-holstered the GP100.

'Reload,' I said, 'take a few extra shells and go cover the windows by the driveway. Stay down and if you see bad guys with guns, shoot them.'

'What're you going to do?'

'Get the guys from the Watchouse,' I said. I took the ammo back from him, shook the spare rounds loose into my jacket pocket and tossed the box aside. 'Go, and stay low.'

He moved off and I checked the internal hallway. The guy in the Swandri wasn't moving and I could hear slow movement beyond him.

'Put your weapon down,' I called out, 'come out with your hands up and nobody will get hurt.'

'Fuck youse,' the guy shouted back. 'I can see you, pigshit. I'll fuckin' kill you!'

'Put your weapon down,' I repeated. The shotgun was at my shoulder, ready to go.

He unleashed another volley of abuse and I saw a shadow moving on the tiled floor. He was coming closer, getting ready to make a move.

I reached slowly and carefully behind me with my left hand, found the wastepaper bin I'd seen, and picked it up. With the shotgun still ready, I tossed the bin through the doorway and it hit the floor with a loud clatter.

There was the sound of a shot as I was up and moving, and I leaped over the guy in the Swandri, slipping on some broken glass as I landed and went down sideways. The front counter was to my right and the guy was crouched down in the middle of the floor, working the bolt of the rifle in his hands.

He looked up as I appeared, and his eyes locked onto mine. He worked the bolt forward, chambering a new round.

I hit the floor on my backside and fired as I went down, squeezing the first trigger and blasting him in the chest. He flopped over backwards with a scream and I sat up, my ears ringing again.

'Watch out!' The voice sounded far away but I knew it came from the Watchouse.

I swivelled on my butt towards the broken front doors, seeing another couple of guys starting to come in. One had a rifle or shotgun in his hands and the other had a length of timber. I fired the second barrel at them, blowing out some more glass and sending them scurrying back into cover.

I scrambled to my feet, broke the shotgun open and reloaded as fast as I could. My hands were trembling but I felt surprisingly calm inside. I backed over to the second guy I'd shot and checked him. The chest of his cheap hoody was very wet and he was staring at the ceiling with open eyes. I felt no remorse at killing him. He was a cop-killer and would happily have killed us too.

I picked up the rifle he'd dropped and backed over to the counter. The other cop appeared and took the gun with bloodied hands. The two Watchouse ladies were huddled beneath a desk and I could hear one of them crying.

I heard the boom of a shotgun and the sound of running feet from Steve's direction.

34

Darroch appeared with his Glock drawn. 'The bastards are coming in the back,' he cried. His eyes were wild and he was breathing hard. I saw that the slide on his pistol was locked open.

'Reload,' I said to him.

He ignored me and looked around, seeing the shot cop at his feet. 'What's wrong with him?'

The other cop scowled. 'He's fuckin' dead! That shithead shot him.'

It seemed a random conversation but I took it as a sign that Darroch was in shock. Steve's shotgun boomed again and I heard glass smashing. Shouts were coming and Steve was shouting back.

'Right,' Darroch said, 'we need a plan.'

'No shit. My plan is to get the fuck out of here,' I said, still watching the front doors.

'We need to defend this station,' Darroch continued. 'We cannot let ourselves be overrun.'

'Can you get hold of your patrols?' I asked.

'No, but I'm hoping they'll turn up.'

'Hope isn't a great plan.'

He scowled. 'They'll hear the shooting and come back in.'

'Unless they don't hear the shooting,' I said, 'or they're tied up with something else. Or they've gone home to look after their families.'

He scowled harder. 'In that case they're cowards and I'll have them arrested.'

I almost laughed. 'Don't be a fuckin' idiot, Dodger. I'm outta here. I suggest you guys do the same.'

I heard Steve's shotgun boom twice in quick succession and I moved in his direction. Getting into the main office I could see him crouched behind a desk, reloading.

'They're down at the meal room,' he called out, 'and I've got no more ammo.' I was pleased to note that he seemed calmer now, his earlier panic gone.

'Come to me,' I said, covering him as he ran across the hallway and got behind me. Together we backed up to the Watchouse. I saw a head poke around the doorframe of the meal room and duck back. I held my fire and joined the others.

'Here's where I leave you,' I said. 'Here.' I kept two spare shells in my pocket and handed the rest to Steve. I glanced at the cop with the rifle. 'You might want to check that guy's pockets for ammo, and I suggest you guys get to the other guns in the exhibit room before they do, if you plan on sticking around.'

Darroch opened his mouth to speak but I cut him off. 'And you probably want to reload, like I told you.'

He looked at his Glock and his cheeks flushed.

'Good luck everybody, I wish you well.'

With that I moved across the front foyer away from the doors. The foyer was encased in floor to ceiling glass and one of the lower panes on the far side had been cracked, probably by shotgun pellets. I hammered it with the butt of the Webley and knocked the glass out, allowing me to squeeze through into a narrow bark garden between the station and the car dealership.

I could hear shouts over the other side of the building but nothing close to me. There was nobody in sight around me, although a few cars were still going past, seemingly oblivious to the carnage in the police station. The truck was across the road and I wasted no time in getting there. I heard a shot behind me and ignored it, just focussed on getting the hell out of there, and within seconds I was in the truck and peeling away from the kerb.

I changed up, working the engine hard, and got my seatbelt buckled with one hand. As I got past the commercial area and started heading out of town, I realised my heart was racing and my hands were trembling.

The after effects of the adrenaline were taking hold, but the good thing was that I felt strangely calm. I had just killed three men and been engaged in both a gunfight and a hand to hand fight, and yet my breathing was coming back to normal and I didn't feel like hurling my guts out.

The trip home was via back roads, circumventing Tuakau town and cutting round the back way through Pukekawa then across the river at Mercer. As I took the motorway overbridge at Mercer I could see a long chain of cars snaking their way south on the highway, moving slowly.

The service centre at Mercer was busy with massive queues of vehicles at the gas station. I saw a brawl on the side of the highway where several cars had collided. One car was spewing steam and another was on its side. Men and women alike were piling into each other, the affray spilling across the highway. As I watched I saw two men grappling together, staggering and swinging fists until one stepped out too far and was clipped by a car crawling past. The driver kept going. I think I would have done too.

The northbound lanes weren't as full but still busy. None of this made me feel any more comfortable.

Looking north as I crossed the motorway overbridge, I could see clouds of smoke in the distance. It looked like Auckland was on fire. I could only hope that Gemma was clear of it already.

Nothing appeared to be amiss when I turned into our road, and as I started up the driveway, I saw the motorhome parked beside the house. I felt my spirits lift immediately, knowing that another part of our family had made it to safety.

Archie came running out when I pulled up and leaped on me, giving me a great big hug that was the best hug in the world and just what I needed. I held him tight, breathed him in and kissed his soft cheek. Jethro came and bumped my legs.

'I missed you, Dad,' Archie said, his skinny arms wrapped around my neck. 'And guess what?'

'What, buddy?'

'Nana and Poppa are here.'

'I bet you're glad to see them.'

He wriggled down and I followed him to the door, where Gemma's parents were waiting. I hugged Sandy and shook hands with Rob. He held onto my hand, scrutinizing me.

'Archie,' he said, 'you take Nana inside for a moment, okay?'

They did so and he released my grip.

'You okay?' he asked, watching me carefully.

I felt a sudden surge of emotion and told him what had happened, trying to keep it as brief as possible. He listened silently but I could tell from his expression that he was shocked. I understood. It wasn't your average day.

When I was finished I took a deep breath and looked at him.

'I'm glad you're safe,' he said quietly. 'It's better that you're home with all of us, and I think we probably need to stay put for a while.' His eyes softened. 'And wait for Gemma to get home.'

An unspoken fear passed between us and I hugged him. Rob wasn't a huggy person but we both needed it right then, and it was good to know I had another reliable man beside me.

It had been a shit day so far and I had the feeling that things weren't going to get any easier.

35

A ctivity on the streets was on the up and none of it was good. Sirens wailed constantly and emergency service vehicles of all three types were frequently racing past. Ellerslie moulded into the fringes of Mt Wellington and Gemma made the decision to follow the main road south. The Ellerslie-Panmure Highway would expose them more, but she reasoned that it was also faster.

It felt risky as hell trying to balance their safety with the need for speed, but while she debated the pros and cons with Alex, it occurred to her that there were only two options. Neither of them was great, so it was actually a simple decision to make.

If they stayed on the main drag there was probably a higher chance of coming across trouble. If they came across trouble in a back street, there was probably less chance of someone intervening to help them. With the memory of the cop-killing thugs so fresh, Gemma determined that she would not hesitate to defend herself again.

They made good time to the next suburb, Panmure, and as they approached it Gemma caught the distinct smell of burning. Straight ahead of them was the Panmure roundabout, a major junction with five roads off it, three of them accessing different suburbs. Left was

Glen Innes and ahead was the Panmure town centre. At two o'clock was the road to Pakuranga, which was where she wanted to go.

The smell of burning got stronger as they came level with the roundabout. It took her a moment to pinpoint the origin, a Vietnamese takeaway store in the town centre with a car crashed through the front of it.

The store was on fire inside and smoke was starting to billow out. The car sounded like it was still revving. People were gathering outside and she could see others carrying goods from an electronics store across the road.

Still a hundred metres or so away, she could tell that trouble was going to erupt properly any minute. An Asian man, presumably from the takeaway store, was on the footpath screaming at the people gathered outside. The smaller group across the road were too busy carrying out TVs and sound systems to be bothered. God only knew what they were planning to do with them right now.

'We need to go around,' Gemma said, pausing to reconsider their options. Alex pulled up beside her, watching the people ahead of them.

'I think there's going to be a fight,' he said.

No sooner had the words left his mouth than a woman from the group stepped out and hit the Asian man with a haymaker. He was knocked on his back, rolled and came up fighting. The woman found herself on her arse and it triggered the rest of the group to pile in on him, fists and feet swinging.

A younger Asian guy and an older woman came from nowhere and jumped in, trying to defend the man.

'We need to get outta here,' Gemma said.

She steered Alex off the footpath into the forecourt of a car yard, ducking down between the vehicles. The Glock was digging into her stomach. They heard smashing glass from the direction of the brawl, accompanied by screaming and shouting.

The car yard was on the corner of a side street and the highway. She could see activity down on Lagoon Drive, the main road that crossed the Panmure Basin on its way to Pakuranga and the nicer suburbs. She knew she would feel safer when she got a bit further south, but the bridge across the water looked like it was blocked by a crash.

Cars were stopped in both directions, horns were honking and people were out on the road. She could hear shouting. More noise was coming from the direction of the brawl outside the shop, and although she could no longer see it, she could hear smashing glass and angry shouts. They needed to get away from that, but she was also wary of the growing incident ahead of them at the bridge.

'This way,' Gemma said.

She led Alex down the side street, away from the roundabout. A set of stone steps led from the houses down to the car park of the leisure centre below, perched on the shore of the lagoon and adjacent to the bridge road.

The car park was still partially full, with a few huddles of people dotted about. Gemma wondered if they had stayed there the night, or come back to collect cars they'd abandoned yesterday. Some watched her and Alex as they crossed the car park, but nobody spoke until they were nearly at the far side, closest to the bridge.

A woman stepped out from the huddle she shared with several other women. They were gathered around a car, smoking and talking in low tones.

'Hey,' she said. 'Where have you come from?'

'The city,' Gemma answered shortly, not breaking her stride.

She was trying to get a better angle on the disorder up ahead. If they couldn't cross the bridge it was going to be a major pain. It would mean cutting around the lagoon itself and crossing over at Waipuna Bridge a little further over, but there were no guarantees that would be any better.

'What's it like in there?' the woman asked.

Gemma paused and looked at her. She was about Gemma's own age, working class, probably a mum. Bleached hair with dark regrowth, chipped nails. Gemma's instinct was to keep moving, not engage with anyone. She had someplace to get to and she didn't have time to waste. But she could see the stress in the woman's face. All she wanted was some information.

'It's pretty bad,' Gemma said. 'People are running wild and there aren't enough cops around to keep a lid on it.'

'Fuckin' pigs,' someone in the group said, and there was a murmur of agreement.

Gemma shot a glance at Alex, who was starting to look uncomfortable. He looked to her for direction.

'We've gotta go,' she said, indicating for him to follow her. She started to move off.

'Where you goin'?' It was another of the group, a Maori in her forties with a fat gut hanging over the front of her black jeans. She stepped out now too, taking a few steps ahead of her mate.

Gemma didn't like the look of her, or the others who were starting to gather behind her.

'Alex,' she said quietly, 'let's go.'

'You got any food?' the leader said. 'We need food for our babies.'

'No.'

'Whatchu got in your bag? Gimme a look in your bag.'

Gemma ignored her and continued walking, moving at an angle to keep them in sight. One was already starting to drift off as if to outflank them, and the atmosphere had changed quickly.

'Gimme your fuckin' bag, bitch.' The Maori woman came forward with her fists bunched. 'You fuckin' slut. I'll fuckin' smash you, cunt. Gimme your bag!'

'Fuckin' smash her, sis,' one of the others cheered. 'Fuckin' slut-whore.'

'Hey, hey.' Alex finally found his voice. 'There's no need for that.'

'Shut up you fuckin' faggot,' the woman responded. 'Fuck up or I'll fuck you up.'

Gemma had had enough and she knew this was a fight they weren't going to win by being timid. As the woman continued coming, Gemma reached under her top and pulled the Glock from her waistband. She raised it in both hands and pointed it straight at the woman's face.

The woman took two more steps before registering what was happening. She stopped short, her mouth moving silently.

'Back off,' Gemma said as firmly as she could. The pistol was trembling in her grip.

'Or what?' the leader said. She stayed where she was, but the threat of the gun wasn't having quite the effect Gemma had thought it would. 'Or what, you fuckin' slut?'

'Or I'll blow your fuckin' head off, arsehole,' Gemma snarled, with a fury that surprised herself.

'Ow, not even,' someone called out.

'You're all shit,' the leader said, sticking out a grubby hand. 'Gimme the fuckin' gun before I fuck you up.'

She stepped forward and Gemma pulled the trigger at the same time.

The shot was loud and frightening, but the effect was immediate. The shot went wide of the leader, cracking past her shoulder and blowing out a side window of the car the group had been gathered around.

The leader shrieked and bolted to the side, her hair flying and her fat gut wobbling. The rest of the group scattered and ran for cover.

Gemma froze for a moment, unsure if she'd hit anyone.

'Come on,' Alex was saying, 'Gemma! Come on, let's go!'

She snapped out of her daze and ran after him, still clutching the Glock. Her ears were ringing and her heart was pounding. Nobody came after them as they reached the road and headed for the bridge.

People were still milling about, seemingly oblivious to the shot that had just been fired. One of the crashed cars had its front stoved in and it was spewing steam from a punctured radiator.

Alex led the way, picking a path around the cars and holding the first aid pack in front of him to make himself as narrow as possible as he tried to get through. As they hurried through a guy stepped in their way, steam swirling around him, and made to grab at Alex.

Without thinking, Alex barged forward with the medical pack as a battering ram, and crashed into the guy front-on. The guy looked surprised and yelped as he was knocked backwards and a second later the two runners were past him, leaving him sprawled and clutching at air.

They got past the crash, around a tussle between two men in the road – presumably the drivers involved in the crash – and were on the other side before they knew it. What had seemed a major obstacle had been overcome in seconds, and they continued running.

Gemma eventually realised she still had the pistol drawn, and shoved it back in her waistband. She noticed that her hand was steady now. Alex ducked off into a side street and bent over with his hands on his knees, wheezing.

She caught up to him and stopped, hands on her hips as she sucked down air. It hadn't been a long run but it was fast and the fear of being caught meant she'd hardly taken a breath.

'Thank God for spin class,' she panted, 'I should've gone more often.'

Alex looked up at her, his face glistening. 'I should've gone at all.'

They both grinned, then a chuckle broke out and in seconds they were laughing hysterically, the tension breaking.

'I gotta say,' Gemma said, getting herself under control, 'I was shitting myself back there. I thought those bitches were gunna kill us.'

Alex straightened up and wiped his eyes on his sleeve. He looked at her quizzically. 'I don't believe that,' he said. 'You were so calm. I would've actually shat myself.'

'I wasn't calm. My hands were shaking so much I thought I was going to drop the gun.' She dug out her water and cracked the lid. 'We were in serious shit there, though. I think they would've killed us.'

She took a drink and wiped her mouth. She realised Alex was still staring at her.

'What?'

'I can't figure you out,' he said. 'I barely know you, like, we hardly ever even talked at work. You don't look any different to anyone else at work.'

'I'm just me,' she shrugged, looking away.

'Yeah but how do you do this?'

'Do what?'

'All this.' He gestured at their surroundings. 'This is not normal, it's not normal at all, but here you are. Running round with a pack on your back and a gun in your hand like you do this every day. Camping under the stars.' He shook his head. 'I don't get it.'

'You keep saying that, but what's not to get? I have a son to get home to, and a family. I need to get home. We go camping, so I know how to do that stuff. My husband's what they call a prepper, which is why I had a bag of gear in the car. He calls it a "get home bag".'

'See, that's not normal. I don't have all that stuff.'

Gemma shrugged again. 'Most people don't, but they probably should. Look, I'm not into it like him, it's his thing. But I know how to fend for myself a bit, and I've shot guns a little bit before, and I have somewhere to go. So here we are.' She gave him an apologetic smile. 'And I'm glad you're here with me.'

'I'm glad I am too. At least you'll protect me.'

'You did alright back there, you got us over the bridge.' Gemma shouldered her bag again. 'Come on, let's go. We're wasting time.'

36

Now that we had a houseful and weren't anticipating any more, we needed to make some defensive preparations.

Rob had moved the motorhome around the back of the house, out of sight of the road, and they were settled in. Relations between them and my mother had been strained for years, but they had always managed a polite civility. The circumstances being different put a whole new spin on it now, and the two women had busied themselves together in the kitchen.

I had set Archie to work with his Lego and collared Rob, taking him to the gun safe and showing him what I had. Being ex-Navy he was familiar with firearms, and I gave him a quick run through all of them. I also gave him the clip chargers and boxes of .303 ammo I had bought. He'd never got round to passing on his old Lee Enfield, but I was pleased I had the ammo anyway.

Rob raised his eyebrows when he saw the Browning, and he gave me a look that was probably disapproving.

'Ask me no questions,' I said, 'and I'll tell you no lies.' I handed the holstered Browning to him. 'Ever fired one before?'

He drew it out and turned it over in his hands. 'This is what we had way back when, but I never used one. Or any pistol, for that matter.'

'Now's as good a time as any to learn.'

I ran him through a crash course on that as well and handed him the spare magazines with it. He looked at the pistol and the magazines and the boxes of .303 and 9mm Parabellum.

'Looks like we're going to war,' he said pensively.

I paused, nodding silently. 'Yeah,' I said finally, not really sure how to answer that. 'It does, doesn't it?'

'Do you think it's that bad?' He looked me in the eye. 'Honestly?'

I paused again. I sensed that a lot rode on the question and how I responded. In the end it was a pretty simple answer.

'I know that it will be tough,' I said carefully. 'I don't know how tough, but whatever comes, I want us to be prepared for it.'

Rob nodded slowly, churning it over. This was a turning point for us. If things turned out not so bad and we over-reacted, there could be legal and social consequences for that. If it turned out real bad and we were unprepared, we could wind up dead.

Both of us got that without needing to articulate it, and we knew we were on the same page. Rob nodded again and threaded the Browning in the pancake holster onto his belt. He slipped the spare magazines into the pockets of his jeans. He drew the pistol, racked the slide and checked the safety. He re-holstered it and hitched up his belt.

'I'm ready, boy,' he said, a steely determination in his voice. 'No bastard's getting past us.'

I nodded. 'Damn right,' I said.

I took the Mossberg and a bandolier of spare ammo out to the hall and placed them in the cupboard near the front door. Rob gathered the ladies and Archie into the lounge and we sat on the couches like we had so many times before. This time there was no coffee and biscuits, no TV, no family birthday to celebrate.

I kicked off what I later came to think of as a council of war.

'Until this thing either blows over or gets sorted, we need to look after ourselves,' I said. 'We're a little bit cramped here but we'll make do. We've got plenty of food and more in the garden, and we can always hunt more if we need to.'

'I don't like rabbits, Dad,' Archie told me, with all the authority of a seven-year-old. 'I've told you that before.'

'That's no problem, wee man,' I said. Now wasn't the time to point out that rabbit stew may well be on the menu in the near future. 'As part of this, we all need to pitch in and do a bit extra. And that means all of us.'

I gave Archie a direct look and he rolled his eyes dramatically.

'Dad, I already put my bag away, set the table, feed the cat, and close my curtains.' He threw his hands up for effect. 'What more can I do?'

'You also help carry in the firewood,' I reminded him, 'and play with the dog. So you are very helpful, aren't you?'

'I know! That's what I've been trying to tell you.' He turned to Sandy beside him. 'He never listens to me, Nana.'

'Well I think we'll manage to keep the kitchen running won't we, Jenny?' said Sandy. 'At least until Gemma gets home, anyway.'

'Of course, I'm sure we will,' my mother agreed, with a feigned show of solidarity. 'And we'll probably need to afterwards, as well.'

I raised an eyebrow and gave her a look. She pretended not to notice, and Sandy let it slide. Too many more of those digs though and there would be fireworks.

'I think while the power is still on to some degree we should make the most of it, and get some of our meat dried and maybe some baking? We can use the dehydrator for some of it.'

'Leave it to us, my son,' my mother said. 'You do your thing.'

I bit my tongue again and carried on.

'We'll get some defences in place,' I said, 'make it a bit harder for any visitors to get up to us. And we'll also visit the neighbours, see who's around and what they're up to. See what everyone's heard. There may be someone with a shortwave radio or something who's got news that we haven't heard.'

With the phone networks out of action, getting information was going to be difficult. Luckily I wasn't of the generation born with a smart phone in their hand; I still knew how to talk to people. I also knew most of the neighbours around here.

I stood, ending the council of war. We had things to do.

37

Although the roads were busy the traffic was moving, and Gemma was keen to get their hands on a vehicle, knowing that it would save them time if they were mobile.

'We could even hitch hike,' Alex suggested, pacing along beside her as they headed southeast on Ti Rakau Drive.

It would take them to Manukau but before they got there they would go through some rough areas and get close to others, and she figured they had a better chance of outrunning trouble in a vehicle than on foot. Plus her feet and legs were feeling it and she knew that Alex would be in worse shape than her – he didn't seem to be very fit and was certainly no kind of outdoorsman. Just her luck to be buddied with someone from IT.

Gemma frowned as she considered his suggestion. She wasn't convinced that hitch hiking was ever a safe option, let alone now.

'We could,' she conceded, 'but I'd probably rather we had control of it.' She gave him a sideways glance. 'You look like you could do with a rest, anyway.'

He'd been favouring his left leg for some time now, but had stayed silent so she figured it probably wasn't too bad. A geek like him probably didn't walk further than the cafeteria.

'I'm okay,' he said.

They walked on, sticking to the footpath and keeping their heads on swivels to avoid any nasty surprises. They weren't the only people on the hoof and there were also a decent number of cyclists on the road, even a few on scooters and skateboards.

Gemma noticed that the behaviour of the traffic had deteriorated. More than just a lack of basic courtesy, drivers were using the wrong side of the road, flying past when they could, mounting kerbs and footpaths to get around hold ups, and generally acting like they were in a Third World country.

Maybe they were, she figured. The thought made her feel sick. The image she kept seeing in her mind's eye was of Archie, smiling and happy, just how a child should be. There was no way he should be growing up in an environment like this. She knew that Mark would be taking good care of him but she needed to get home.

She jumped when she felt a hand on her arm, and realised Alex was speaking to her. He wore a pained expression.

'I need to stop,' he said. 'I think there's something wrong.'

She pulled up. 'With what?'

'My foot, it's killing me.'

Gemma looked around, seeking somewhere safe to stop. They may as well throw up a neon VICTIM sign by tending to an injury on the side of the road. She spotted a small commercial block a hundred metres or so ahead.

'Up there,' she said.

He hobbled beside her until they got there. It was a double-storey suburban office block that housed an accounting practice, an investment adviser and a property conveyancing practice on the ground floor, the business names plastered across the plate glass windows at street level. All three businesses were locked up with the blinds drawn and lights off. She couldn't see what was upstairs, but the windows there were also covered.

Nobody responded to knocking at the front doors so they went around the back. It was a small parking area with a dumpster and loose rubbish. The back doors were also locked.

'What're you doing?' Alex said, as Gemma rummaged in her bag.

She produced a small pry bar and stood up. 'We'll be safer inside.'

'You can't just break in,' he protested. 'Isn't your husband a police officer?'

She went to the closest door, being the lawyers'. 'We need to get off the street so we can have a look at your foot and sort you out.'

She got the slim bar into the gap and leaned into it. Conveyancing may have made good money, but the manager needed to invest some of it in their office security. The door popped open on her second go and she led the way in. She saw an alarm panel on the wall but there were no power lights showing. She flicked a switch for the main lights but nothing happened.

'Power's out,' she said.

'Probably either the grid has gone down, or possibly a localised outage,' Alex said.

They came through a small kitchenette into the reception area, and he eased himself down onto a sofa. He began unlacing his shoe while Gemma checked that they were alone. Upstairs was the main office, an open plan affair with three desks. Downstairs was the boss' office, a larger room with better furnishings than those for the workers.

She returned to the reception to find Alex had his shoe and sock off and was examining his foot. He had a decent blister on his heel that was intact, and one on his big toe, which had rubbed raw.

'Jesus,' she said, 'no wonder you couldn't walk. How long's it been like that?'

'Since yesterday.'

Gemma's respect for him shot up several notches. He'd not said a word about it that whole time. She took back her earlier thoughts about his lack of physical abilities.

'What're you like with first aid?' she asked.

'I did a course a few years ago.' He looked embarrassed. 'They made me the Health and Safety rep for the IT department. I had to do a refresher each year, although I did miss the last one.' He gave a goofy grin. 'Our main frame went down and I had to work through...' He saw her blank look. 'Anyway, I know what to do with a blister.'

'Good,' she said. 'I'm going to look around.'

She took the torch from her daypack and used it to poke around the boss' office. She didn't know what she expected to find, but hopefully there would be something of use to them on their journey. Alex's reaction to her breaking in was right but she reasoned that, given the current circumstances, a degree of legal leniency could be applied.

She wasn't disappointed. The boss kept a supply of sweets in his desk and she took them. He also had a small beer fridge hidden in a cabinet, which housed bottles of water and cans of full-fat Coke in addition to his craft beers. The fridge wasn't running but the bottles were still cool. She stacked some by the door to come back to, and went upstairs.

The three workers were obviously younger than the boss, judging by the photos and paraphernalia on their desks. One had two protein bars in his desk drawer, as well as packets of instant noodles and canned tuna. The standard quick-fix lunch of the office rat. The second had a wide selection of herbal teas but nothing else, and the third only had cigarettes. She took the lighter with them but left the smokes and the teas.

A cupboard under the front window was home to stationery and personal belongings. One of the workers was a runner – she guessed probably not the smoker – and in one section of the cupboard was a daypack with a change of running kit and a pair of trainers on top of it.

Gemma took the trainers and socks downstairs with her, along with the food supplies, and showed them to Alex. He stopped taping his foot long enough to check them.

'They're a size too big,' he said. 'I'm only a nine.'

'Try them on anyway,' she said. She caught his look. 'We can leave a note if you like and you can sort it out later. But your shoes are obviously no good for the amount of walking we're doing.'

'Let me sort this out,' he said, obviously not wanting to argue. He turned his attention back to his foot.

'I'm going next door,' she said.

She repeated the process on the accountancy practice next door, finding nothing of any real use to them. The last stop was the investment adviser's office, and there she struck gold.

Not only was there a snack box in the foyer, but the upstairs office had a wardrobe. Judging by the fold out sofa bed and the amount of clothes in the wardrobe, Gemma guessed that someone spent at least a couple of nights a week there.

She rummaged through the wardrobe and found a full set of casual clothes that were close enough to Alex's size. She bundled them up and went back downstairs to the snack box. Crackers, cookies, chocolate and protein bars, candy, microwave rice and fruit sticks; it all went into a plastic shopping bag she found behind the receptionist's desk.

'Here,' she said to Alex, dumping the clothes on the sofa beside him. 'A rain jacket, T shirts, jeans, a hoody, a cap and shorts. And,' she said, triumphantly holding up a pair of trainers, 'size nines.'

This time he didn't even argue.

By the time Alex had changed into the shorts and trainers, a new T shirt and fresh socks, Gemma had divided up the rest of the supplies. She downed a can of Coke and shoved another one into her day pack, along with bottled water and as much of the food supplies as she could fit. It was very full and heavy now and she heaved it onto her back.

Alex filled his own bag up and shouldered it, and dumped his old clothes into the bin.

'Not much use to me now,' he said, draining a water bottle and binning it as well.

'Are you okay to go?'

'Yep.' He gave a firm nod. 'Let's go.'

Gemma opened the rear door, glancing back at him. 'You coming?'

'Thanks,' he said. 'For looking after me.'

'We're looking after each other,' she told him. 'Now let's get moving.'

38

The van Dijks were home when we crossed the road and called on them.

The old man, Rusty – on account of his wiry red hair – answered the door in his slippers with a smile on his face. He was a rake of a man with a pronounced Adam's apple.

'Sho nice to shee you, Mark,' he said with his heavy accent. 'Where ish da little one?'

'He's at home,' I said, shaking his hand. 'You remember Rob?'

'Of coursh, of coursh. Good to shee you, my friend.'

They shook hands too, then Sophie came out and kissed me on both cheeks. Rusty's wife was one of those portly women who always wore two things – an apron and rosy cheeks.

'Terrible newsh, ishn't it?' she said. 'How ish Gemma doing?'

'She's still on the way home,' I said. Her face fell. 'But I'm sure she'll be fine,' I added quickly.

'Come in, come in,' Rusty said, ushering us into their lounge.

Framed photos of their kids and grandkids were everywhere and there was an old bolt action .22 leaning by Rusty's armchair.

'Been potting rabbits, Rusty?' Rob said with a smile.

'Shomething like that, yesh.' Rusty squared his shoulders. 'I shaw thoshe thieves at your houshe, Mark. I shaw you run them off.'

'He did, you know,' Sophie agreed. 'He wash out there with hish rifle, ready to shoot those buggersh if they gave you any trouble, Mark.'

I turned to Rob. 'Neighbourhood Watch, country style.'

We stayed and talked for a while, learning that the van Dijks planned on staying put and riding out the situation. Two of their kids lived in Auckland and the other was in Australia, and they hoped to hear from them soon. Having tried calling and texting Gemma earlier, with no luck, I didn't hold out much hope for them.

Rusty walked us to the door and shook hands again.

'Take care of yourshelfsh, you two. And dat little one. He'sh a cheeky one, you know.' His eyes sparkled. 'I never told you Mark, but I caught him pinching plumsh off my tree. He got such a fright, he thought I wash going to tell on him to hish dad.'

I smiled, because I already knew. It had happened a month ago and Archie had told Gemma the same day, asking her not to tell me.

'I hope you tanned his backside and sent him home, Rusty,' Rob said with a chuckle.

'No, no, dere wash no need. I shent him on hish way and told him to come back tomorrow for shome more.'

'Take care, Rusty,' I said. 'Pop over when you want, otherwise we'll probably drop in again tomorrow.'

'Keeping an eye on de old folksh, Mark?' His eyes sparkled again.

I shrugged. 'We all need to look out for each other right now,' I said.

'We do, we do.' He clapped us both on the back and we headed off to the next house down from ours.

The Macklin house was set well back from the road and had large black wrought iron gates that were closed. They were a wealthy family and had a tennis court beside the house. The parents lived there with the youngest kid, the older one being off at university in Otago.

I couldn't see any movement at the house, and hadn't seen them for a few days. It was possible they were at their beach house, or maybe they were just hunkered down. If they were away the farm would have continued running anyway, with their workers who lived further down taking care of business.

A couple of horses in the front paddock watched us as we rattled the gate and called out. One shook away a fly and blinked at us. The other took a dump. Neither seemed to be bothered by us.

'Try them again tomorrow,' Rob said.

I joined him at the shoulder of the road, looking both ways down the asphalt. No vehicles or people were in sight.

'All quiet on the Western Front,' Rob said.

I nodded. 'For now,' I said.

We headed back home, discussing what security arrangements we could make. The timber and other bits and pieces I had picked up from Mitre 10 hadn't been put to use yet, but between us we had some ideas of what to do. The burglars and the incident at the cop station had hardened my resolve that we needed to be prepared for things to get much worse, and I was thinking of constructing a safe room of some sort.

I was explaining this to Rob in the shed when Archie ran in, interrupting the conservation.

'Dad, someone's coming up the drive.'

He tugged at my sleeve but I was already moving, Rob just behind me. From the shed door I could see a man and a woman walking towards the house.

'It's the neighbours,' I said. 'You guys wait inside.'

They weren't openly carrying firearms, but I kept the Ruger Magnum on my belt just in case.

Brenton and Linda Rees lived further down the road, maybe half a klick away, on a small lifestyle block. Hobby farmers who both worked in Auckland, they drove the requisite SUV and kept chooks, because that's what everyone in their circle did. I'd met them in passing a few times. They had two kids, both in schools down in Hamilton.

I met them at the top of the drive.

'Boy, are we glad to see you,' Brenton said with a relieved smile. We shook hands and Linda gave me a strained, nervous smile. 'This is some strange times, right?'

I nodded. Strange was not quite how I'd put it. Strange meant you didn't know what to make of it. I knew what to make of it, alright.

'Sure is,' I said. 'How're you guys getting on?'

'We're not too bad, we've not been to work though,' Linda said.

I felt my eyebrows raise at that but I said nothing. It made sense to have allies at the moment rather than piss people off.

Picking up on my reaction, she added, 'But we've got the kids home, so thank God they're safe.'

'Is Hamilton having the same issues as up here?' I said, and Brenton nodded vigorously.

'Hell yeah,' he said. 'We raced down there and got them, took us three hours to get to school and damn near five to get back.'

I knew it was normally about an hour each way. I quizzed them on what they'd seen down there and it was the same, but on a larger scale, as what I'd seen in Pukekohe – civil unrest. Roads jammed with people fleeing the city. Emergency services battling to cope. Stores emptied of goods. People fighting in the streets.

'We even heard gunshots,' Brenton said, giving an involuntary shudder.

Linda looked to him. 'Which leads us here...'

He looked uncomfortable, but with his wife alongside, he had no choice but to ask.

'Yeah, Mark...so, I know you're a bit of a hunter...' he said.

Linda nudged him with her elbow.

'The thing is,' he said, 'I can't see this thing getting any better soon, right? I mean, people were shooting down in Hamilton, and I'm sure Auckland will be the same, maybe even around here, right?'

You have no fuckin' clue, I thought to myself. If only he knew what my day had been like, he'd shit his pants.

'The thing is,' he continued, 'we might need to defend ourselves, right? I mean, I've got Linda and the kids, you know?'

'True.' I nodded.

'And, you know, I mean I know you're a hunter and all that...'

'Spit it out,' I said, tired of his fumbling. 'What are you asking me?'

'I don't have a gun,' he said, the words coming out in a rush. 'I was wondering if maybe you'd be able to, you know...'

Linda was obviously as tired of it as I was. 'Can you lend us a gun?' she said. 'At least until things sort themselves out? Please?'

The desperation and anxiety in their faces was very real, and I could understand why. These were average people caught up in a situation they were not equipped for. A situation they never dreamed would happen to them. They were not me.

Non-preppers had always thought of preppers as negative people, doomsayers who almost willed something bad to happen so they could run to their bunker, arm up and start eating freeze-dried meals.

The reality was far different.

Yeah, there are nutcases in every sector of society, but the difference between people like me and people like the Rees' was that while they went through life with a happy smile on their face; I went through it with a happy smile on my face and one eye on the shadows.

I looked for the monsters because I knew they were there. I prepared for the unexpected because I expected it to happen sometime. None of that stopped me from living a good, happy life. But it did mean that right now, when shit was going down, I wasn't caught short like these guys.

'I mean, it's not like we want to shoot anyone, right? But, you know...I mean, you've gotta be prepared, right?'

I murmured my agreement while I considered their request. Every gun I had was for a particular purpose. The .22 was for shooting rabbits and the odd feral cat that strayed across my path. The shotgun was for possums and ducks. The lever action Rossi was for anything mid-sized – goats or pigs, mostly.

The pistols I would be keeping quiet about – even though they had seen the Ruger on my hip – and they were strictly for self-defence, not assault. Rob's rifle was his and I couldn't speak for him.

The danger in giving a weapon to an untrained, unskilled amateur was that they were likely to hurt themselves or someone else by accident. Or use it as the first option rather than the last resort. But I did get where they were coming from, and they were right. If my neighbours were capable of defending themselves then that made us safer.

'Wait here.'

I went inside and fetched the sawn-off Webley and Scott. I handed a box of #4 birdshot rounds to Linda, and showed Brenton how to break the weapon open. A quick lesson on safety and how to load, aim and fire and they were good to go. They thanked me over and over and promised to get it back to me.

'Keep it,' I said, 'it's not mine anyway.'

Brenton gave me a curious look. 'What d'you mean?'

'Don't worry about it. You guys take care, I'll come down and check on you in a day or two maybe, eh?'

'Be careful,' Linda grinned, trying hard to be jovial, 'he's armed and dangerous now.'

Brenton grinned too and hefted the shotgun in his hands. 'That's right, armed and dangerous, right?'

'Just remember where you're pointing that thing,' I said. 'And one more thing.'

They looked at me expectantly.

'Don't go telling anyone you got that from me, okay? I don't want every man and his dog turning up here wanting me to help them.' I looked from one to the other. 'Are we clear on that?'

'Sure, sure.' They both nodded.

Rob and Archie sidled up beside me. Together we stood and watched them head off back down the driveway, Brenton holding the sawn-off shotgun carefully.

'You sure that was a wise move?' the older man said.

I hiked my shoulders. 'Dunno. I hope so.'

'He know what to do with that thing?'

'More than he did.' I turned to him. 'I don't think he's any better shooter than my mother, Rob, but now he owes me a favour. That can't be a bad thing.'

He gave a slow nod. 'Fair enough.' He shifted his eyes from the disappearing couple and looked me in the eye. 'I suspect this thing, whatever it is, is going to mean more people will need to pick up a gun.'

I nodded my agreement.

His tone softened and he swallowed. 'I hope my girl makes it home safely.'

I nodded again. The twist of dread in my gut weighed heavy.

39

Once Alex had sorted his feet out and got a comfortable pair of shoes on, they made good time. They were refreshed after a short rest and had food and water in their bellies.

Gemma had rearranged her gear again, making a bed roll with a tarp and blanket and securing that to the bottom of her bag. Having it across the top would have restricted her access to the top-opening bag, which she had refilled with her share of the food and water they had scrounged.

They had also stripped down the medical kit and taken the items they thought they were most likely to need, sharing them out between themselves and leaving the rest of the kit behind. She hoped they would be more mobile with one less bag to carry.

The Glock was tucked into Gemma's waistband and the spare magazine was in her pocket.

Setting off from the suburban businesses they set a cracking pace that took them along the main highway of Ti Rakau Drive from Pakuranga to Botany. Traffic was heavier and it seemed to Gemma that the mood in the air was getting more tense.

Every gas station they saw had signs up, but the signs differed.

The only stations that still had power had more than quadrupled their prices, but still had a queue a mile long. The other stations had cars coming in and ducking out again once they saw the signs stating NO GAS.

A brawl between two opposing groups outside a burger joint caused Gemma and Alex to run past, having no interest in getting caught up in a fight. Up ahead was a major junction with sets of shops on each of the four corners. It was busy on a normal day but today was chaos. The traffic lights were out and the roads were jammed, people trying to get in to the two supermarkets – Countdown on the northern side, closest to Gemma and Alex, and Pak'n'Save on the opposite side.

A pair of yahoos on pit bikes were racing around, weaving in and out of the traffic, taking the opportunity to smash wing mirrors off cars with pieces of pipe as they went past. A Police car was on the footpath across the road, both cops standing beside it wearing body armour and brandishing M4s. Watching what was going on, they made no move to intervene.

'What are they waiting for?' Alex wondered aloud. 'Why don't they do something?'

'What can they do?' Gemma said.

She kept a wary eye on the two bikes. The riders were keeping their distance but jeering at the cops, egging them on to do something. Gemma was pretty sure what Mark would have wanted to do if he was in their shoes.

She wondered if she could approach the cops for help, but there seemed little point. They couldn't get anywhere in this traffic anyway, even if they were available to help. She paused to consider their options.

'TI Drive or Chapel Road?' she said. 'What d'you think?'

'Chapel Rd,' Alex said without hesitation. 'It's probably quieter.'

She knew he was right. Te Irirangi Drive was another urban highway, a long double-lane road that went all the way to Manukau. A block further south, Chapel Rd ran parallel, but was more suburban and a little further from the crime-ridden 'hood of Otara. Cutting through Dannemora, it also ended up at Manukau, but the parks and greenbelts should give them more opportunity for cover if they needed it.

Decision made, they trotted across the junction past all the stationary cars. Gemma realised that many of them had been abandoned. She could see the frustration in the faces of many people they passed, and she felt for them. At least she and Alex were making ground. Who knew when these people would get home?

To save time they cut across the car park of Botany Town Centre, which was also bedlam. Several cars had been smashed up and she could see a group of young thugs rifling through some of them. She steered Alex wider, putting on a trot to get distance, and soon they were jogging down Chapel Rd.

Gemma knew that Dannemora was a mixed bag of good working people and not so good people. Mark had always said he would never live there because it had a high percentage of rental properties. Rentals attracted criminals, so you never knew who was going to be moving in next door. Sure enough, they soon saw signs of this. The first house in a side street had a bunch of cars haphazardly parked on the road, footpath and front lawn. She recognised gang colours on several of the thugs she saw outside, and a car stereo was booming out some kind of nonsensical bass.

Bottles were being passed around and she could see broken glass on the road. The partygoers saw the two joggers passing by and yahooed, but made no move towards them. Gemma picked up the pace, her heart thumping in her chest. Resting one hand on the butt of the Glock in her waistband, she ran hard for a block before easing up, her lungs hankering for a break.

'Jesus,' Alex panted behind her, 'slow down.'

She dropped to a walk and checked behind them. Nobody was following. Vehicles were still going past but nobody stopped. Some people were outside their houses and she saw a few packing up their cars.

A small block of shops up ahead had every front window broken. Shattered glass covered the footpath. A small group of Indian men were gathered outside, one each standing in the doorway of the neighbouring liquor store and dairy.

Each man in the group carried a bat or length of wood. One gripped a hammer and another even held a carving knife. They were jabbering excitedly to each other in their language and one was waving his arm back down the road. Gemma guessed they were talking about the thugs around the corner, who were presumably responsible for the damage to the shops.

The men stopped talking when they saw the two walkers approaching. Gemma raised her hands and tried to look non-threatening as she stepped onto the road and cut around them. The men eyed them menacingly but said nothing. As soon as Gemma and Alex had gone past, the group of men set off in the opposite direction, leaving the two guards behind.

'Hey, wait up.'

Gemma turned. Alex was looking back at the shops, something obviously on his mind.

'You think we should get some food and stuff?' he said.

Gemma hesitated. It wasn't a bad idea, given they had no idea how long it would take to get home, but she also didn't want to get caught up in the drama that was obviously about to happen.

'We'd have to be quick,' she said. 'Are they even open?'

Alex approached the man standing guard outside the dairy. After a short conversation and Alex showing the guy that he had cash, they were allowed inside.

'Hurry,' the guard said. 'You don't wanna be here soon.'

'Did you get robbed?' Alex asked.

The guard nodded. 'They beat up my cousin in the liquor store. My aunty was in here and they beat her up too.' His dark eyes glittered and he hefted the hockey stick in his hand. 'They are going to learn a lesson.'

It was all the impetus that Gemma and Alex needed. The shelves were almost empty and a lot of stock was scattered across the floor, but they managed to find crackers, biscuits, lighters and a few batteries. Gemma found that the hygiene supplies were largely untouched and she took toothbrushes and paste, roll-on deodorant, soap, sunscreen and tampons. She met with Alex at the checkout and they pooled their cash, which was just shy of forty dollars.

The guard ran an eye over the goods and took all the cash, waving them away as he pocketed the money. They moved past the shops before stopping and cramming all the goods into their bags. Alex had carried less to start with so he filled his bag with most of the food.

They carried on, making good time on the long road until they reached the northern fringes of Manukau itself. The bag was heavy on Gemma's shoulders, but it was satisfying to know that they had enough food for a couple of days.

The housing was denser now and they tracked upwards, sticking to the footpath on their way up a hill to Redoubt Rd. To their left it went rural and meandered south. To their right it ran down to Manukau City Centre. The Police district headquarters was down there, as well as the courthouse and the main Westfield shopping centre.

Straight ahead of them, Everglade Drive was a steep drop down through a residential area, heading south towards the sprawling mass of Totara Park and the Botanical Gardens. That was the way they wanted to head; Alex's home was in The Gardens on the other side. They were only a few k's walk from it now.

Gemma could see smoke rising from the direction of Manukau centre, and the smell of burning was heavy in the air. Turning further she could see more smoke from the direction they had come and back towards downtown Auckland. There were so many columns of smoke now they were combining into a single wide cloud that hung over the city. It was like the place had been bombed.

The lights at the intersection they had reached were out and a light delivery truck was stuck through a fence.

'Can you drive a truck?' she asked Alex, and his eyes lit up.

'I can give it a go.'

They waited for a few cars to go past and started to cross the road, but were only halfway through the intersection when she heard and saw movement on the other side of the truck. She grabbed Alex's arm and veered to the left, towards the opposite side.

'What?' he said loudly, caught by surprise.

'Keep going,' she hissed.

A head popped around the rear of the truck to investigate the noise then ducked back. As they came level on the other side of Everglade, they saw what looked like a family pillaging the truck. The parents were carrying armloads of parcels into the property the truck had crashed into, while six or seven teens were unloading the back of it.

They saw the travellers and stopped momentarily.

'What the fuck are you lookin' at?' a teenage boy shouted.

The parents stopped at the front doorstep and put their parcels down, looking back. They were a bogun family – sleeveless T-shirts and singlets, snap back hats, black jeans, lots of hair and tattoos. A pair of dogs were with the younger ones at the roadside.

'Keep walking,' Gemma muttered, one eye on the humans and one on the dogs. Both dogs had pricked their ears up. One was a big bull mastiff, the other a pit bull. Both had studded collars and looked fierce.

'Fuck off or I'll fuck you up, you fuckin' faggot,' one of the girls shouted at them. She was a skanky looking piece with her fat midriff showing beneath a ripped T-shirt. Her hair was streaked with puke green. 'Fuckin' nosey cunts.'

'Watch the dogs,' Gemma muttered.

They kept moving and she was pretty sure they were clear, then one of the dogs bolted. It was the mastiff, a burly beast with a head like a boulder. Its teeth were bared and it was onto the road in a flash.

Alex let out a yelp of alarm and made to run. Gemma stepped back, grabbing at the Glock as the big dog bore down on them. She could hear shouting in the distance but all her attention was on the dog that had zeroed in on Alex and was going for him. It was big enough to knock him over and she could only imagine what it would do if it got him down.

'Call it off!' she screamed, getting the Glock out and extending her arms in a two-handed grip.

The bogun family were still shouting but the dog never flinched. It was almost at the grass verge when she fired. The first round went wide but was enough to distract the dog from Alex. It hesitated, locking onto Gemma instead, and its ears went back. At the same time as the dog came for her Gemma fired, squeezing the trigger three times in quick succession.

She saw two shots ping off the asphalt in front of it but the third impacted the dog's torso and it jerked, stopped, howled and turned and ran. It circled in the middle of the road, craning its neck to lick at its wound, and she became aware of some of the boguns now running towards her.

The mastiff was howling like crazy and flopped onto the road. The people kept coming and she realised that one of the boys, a teenager with an AC/DC T-shirt over his no-chest, was waving a hammer over his head.

Gemma backtracked, her legs wobbling beneath her, her vision completely filled by the guy with the hammer. She could see his mouth moving but couldn't hear a thing over the ringing in her ears from the gunshots. Spit was flying from his lips and his eyes were raging wide, and he was coming for her.

She felt her trigger finger close again and the Glock bucked in her hands. As the barrel dropped down again and the gun smoke wisped away she saw the guy reeling back, a look of complete shock on his face. The hammer was spinning away, end over end, and a second later the guy was following it.

He went down on his back, legs up in the air, twisted and went flat on his back. She saw blood on his chest and he was grabbing at it, pulling his knees up towards his torso.

Gemma stared at him, watching in slow motion as the surreal scene unfolded in front of her. The guy wasn't making a noise but the dog was whining and whimpering. Another sound cut in through the buzz in her head.

'Gemmalookout!'

She snapped her head up, seeing two more boguns bearing down on her. A fat female with yellow/brown hair and an unshaven guy with a snap brim cap and a dog chain in his hand. They were only a few metres away when she punched the Glock towards them in a two-handed grip.

'Fuck off!' she snarled, her ferocity surprising even her. 'Fuck off or I'll shoot you!'

The guy's eyes widened and he staggered, cutting to the side and doubling over as he ran away. The girl was too heavy and uncoordinated to follow suit. Instead of ducking aside she lost her balance, fell on her fat arse and tumbled like a toppled baby.

'Come on!'

Alex was screaming at her and she turned, realising he was right beside her and pulling on her arm.

She went with it, leaving the carnage behind them as they sprinted away down the hill. Alex tripped and tumbled head over heels on the footpath, but got straight back up and carried on running. Gemma's legs moved without conscious effort and she was acutely aware of everything around them – screams and shouts behind them, a car racing by in the opposite direction, birds in the trees of a house they ran past. The warmth of the afternoon sun. The light breeze on her skin. The smell of cordite filling her nostrils.

They crossed side streets and kept going until they reached the end of the road where the hill bottomed out. The expanse of the Botanical Gardens' open green fields was straight ahead and the heavily wooded hills of Totara Park were to their left.

Alex kept going into the green and Gemma followed on, slowing down to catch her breath. Her lungs were heaving and her pulse was slamming but she didn't feel panicked. She called out twice before Alex slowed and looked back. She held the Glock out and he took it like he was taking a scorpion.

'What d'you want me to do with this?' he said.

Gemma moved off the path to the grass. 'Hold it,' she said, tucking back a loose strand of hair, 'I'm just going to throw up.'

40

Back up the road, the family gathered over the fallen youth.

'You dumb fuck,' Curtis Green said, shaking his head. 'Why'd you have to go and do that?'

His wife looked at him, her lip curling. 'He's your fuckin' flesh an' blood,' Lena said. 'Got your fuckin' genes.'

Curtis glowered as he looked down at his nephew. 'He ain't got the brains of my side,' he said. 'Get him up and back inside.'

His two sons, Gunner and Tyson, picked their cousin up under his arms, causing him to cry out in pain. It was a wet, gurgling cry and blood trickled down his chin and onto his throat. His other two kids, the ones who had been shot at by the crazy bitch with the gun, were tending to the wounded dog and looking pissed off.

Carley, fat like her mother but with the stupid impulsiveness of youth, and Zane, as thick as he thought he was smart – which was a lot. Between them they caused him more headaches than anyone ever had. They were from his first missus, not Lena, and were only supposed to be staying a few days. The sooner they fucked off back to her the better, far as Curtis was concerned. Now they'd gone and fucked up again.

'Get that fuckin' mutt off the road,' he growled. 'Go an' sort your shit out.'

'He's really hurt, Dad,' Carley whined. She was cradling the dog's head and crying, making black streaks down her cheeks.

'Well fuckin' sort it out before I shoot the fucker myself,' Curtis snapped.

She started to object but thought better of it, knowing he wasn't joking. She and her brother picked the dog up between them and lugged him across the road, managing to drop him twice before they got him inside.

Curtis looked at Lena and they both rolled their eyes.

'You two.' Curtis looked to the other boy and his sister. 'Go and find where those two cunts have gone.'

Cody nodded hard, her jaw set. She had thin lips and black eyeliner and a rose tattoo on her neck. Dice was the oldest brother but he was retarded – their mother had drunk way too much piss when she was carrying him and taken too many beatings from the old man, not to mention the beatings Dice had taken himself.

The old man was long gone but Dice was still there, as fucked as he was. The youngest, Jaysin, watched them weakly as his cousins carried him towards the house.

'Whaddaya want us to do with them?' Cody said. 'You want us to fuck them up?'

Cody was good at that, but Dice was better. He'd got off every charge he'd ever faced because of his mental disabilities, but she knew damn well he knew what he was doing. He was psychotically violent and he had killed another kid while still at school. These days his talents were often used by their uncle and aunt when low level dealers were fucking them about.

'No.' Lena was emphatic. 'Find out where they are and come tell us.' She gave a cruel sneer. 'We'll go fuck them up ourselves, eh hon?'

Curtis had been staring down the road as if he could see where the man and woman had run to. He turned to her now, his hard gaze meeting hers. For a big man his eyes were abnormally small. He studied his wife for a moment then turned his head, spat, and looked back at his niece and nephew.

'Just find 'em,' he rasped. 'Go.'

As the two youngsters raced off down the street, Lena said, 'He better be okay.'

Curtis took a deep breath and gave his wife a thoughtful look. 'He's gunna die,' he said. 'If he hasn't already.'

Lena felt a kick in her chest. He was so hard that it sometimes even scared her. Years in jail had hardened him beyond repair and she knew he had killed at least two men.

One had been a street bashing when he was just a teenager, and the jury had bought his argument of provocation. The other had been a West Auckland meth dealer only a few years ago. He'd tried to source his gear from another supplier and in the process had bad-mouthed Curtis Green.

Curtis had fixed that by ramming a bayonet through the guy's head. Lena knew all about that one because she'd helped him dump the body in a swamp where, as far as they knew, he still was.

'What'll you tell your brother?' Lena said.

Curtis' lip curled. 'That his son was a fuckin' knucklehead who took a hammer to a fuckin' gunfight.' He put a hand on her back and ushered her towards the house. 'Come on, we got shit to do.'

41

The afternoon had passed slowly, even though I was flat out busy.

I'd checked our property again, thrashed out some plans with Rob, checked on the van Dijks, checked on the ladies who were busy in the kitchen, checked on Rob who was playing Bingo Zingo with Archie. Everyone was fine, everything was secure.

I climbed up and checked the water tank. I checked the food supplies.

Checking, checking, checking. Everything seemed okay, but I was so wired I kept going. I grabbed out my backpack, emptied it and packed it up again. If we needed to bug out for some reason, I wanted to be good to go. I did the same with the small bug out bag I kept for Archie. In the garage cupboard with our two bags was a third – Gemma's.

It was a backpack like mine, a rugged, hard wearing 65-litre pack that carried enough gear for her for three days. Clothes, shelter, lighting, first aid gear, food and water, heating. In the event the shit ever hit the fan, we were good to go. We could drive out or walk out, didn't matter which. We had always hiked as a family and Archie was well used to the great outdoors.

Each of our cars had a similar set up, and I ran a mental checklist over the contents of the get-home bag in Gemma's car. It was enough to last her 24 hours. It had now been a day and a half and she wasn't home.

No messages had come through on any of our phones, there was nothing new on the radio, and I had no idea where she was. What she was doing. If she was okay.

I lifted Archie's BOB into the cupboard and sat back on my haunches. The weight on my shoulders was oppressive. I closed the cupboard door and stood, my knees cracking as I straightened up. I was happy enough that we were okay where we were, at least for now. The burglars of last night bothered me but if they were stupid enough to come back they'd get another dose. I hoped they didn't.

Gemma worried me. She was a smart lady, determined and stubborn to a fault. Resilient. I knew that, wherever she was, she'd be busting a gut to get home. The sooner the better.

Standing there in the silence of the garage, with only my thoughts for company, I made a decision. Now that Rob was there, the rest of the family would be safe at home.

If Gemma wasn't home soon, I would hit the road and look for her.

42

The Gardens was the more upmarket area of Manurewa, an enclave of prosperity in one of the poorest, high crime areas of Auckland.

This was where double-income white collar families lived when they worked in the south side, driving their Jeeps and Land Rovers, sending their kids off on the train to the private schools in the city, avoiding the slums by jumping on the motorway to visit their friends in Howick or do their shopping at Botany or Sylvia Park, before returning home and turning left, not right, away from the ghetto where the great unwashed staggered through their days.

It had always seemed an oddity to Gemma, an oasis of upper middle class in a desert of misery. But right now, she wasn't complaining. Leaving the wounded dog and the probably-dead bogun and the rest of their crew behind them, she and Alex had jogged through the park, making a beeline for his home.

They saw other people in the park, heard some up in the bush, saw some hoons racing about on dirt bikes further away. Gemma prayed that they made it through the park unmolested – she had had enough of other people's shit for one day, or even a life time.

Never had she ever considered the thought that she may one day be fighting for her life. That was Mark's world, a place where, as he liked to say, hard men did bad things so good people could sleep safely at night. It was a world she had glimpsed into, that she was painfully aware of, but that she had never wanted to inhabit.

As she ran, she wondered what he was doing right at that moment. Probably organising everyone like they were his private army, rallying the troops and making sure they were all safe and prepared. *Prepared.*

Had she been prepared for the events of the last two days? On the plus side, she had some gear and she had a rough plan and she was executing it. She had to admit, so far she was doing okay. She was alive and still moving towards home.

Of course, she was pretty sure she'd killed two men, and probably a dog too. The realisation of that weighed on her, but she wasn't falling apart. It hadn't kept her awake last night; in fact, she'd fallen asleep fast. She knew she'd dreamed about it though because she remembered snatches of the dreams, remnants of strong emotions – terror and anger, mostly.

Terror because she thought they were going to get killed. Anger at the thugs who had caused the incident, who had killed the two cops – no, *executed* the two cops – and who had caused her to defend her and Alex. Now it had happened again today, twice. Twice in the space of one day she'd been forced to pull the trigger to defend herself. And the day wasn't over yet.

How dare they? She was a middle-class mother, a member of the school PTA, a mum who watched her son's soccer from the side lines every Saturday, who baked and did crafts, who visited her aging parents and ran around after everyone and always had a "to-do" list a mile long. She wasn't some Terminator woman who ran around getting into gunfights and breaking into buildings and running for her life.

The absurdity of it made Gemma almost laugh.

She realised that Alex was slowing down as they reached the exit from the park. The internal access road came out onto Charles Prevost Drive, the main thoroughfare through The Gardens, and she could see activity. Cars going past, people bustling about at a few houses. Youngsters on bikes – not youngsters from The Gardens though. These were hood rats from the bad side, clearly up to no good. She wasn't surprised.

'Wait up,' Gemma said, grabbing the back of Alex's bag to stop him.

'We're nearly there,' he said impatiently. 'It's just round the corner.'

'Look.' She pointed at the hood rats on their bikes, watching as they circled lazily in the road, scanning the area. One pulled a wheelie down the footpath on the other side.

'So what?'

Gemma saw a family station wagon in a driveway a few houses down, the doors left open as a man lugged bags out from the house and loaded the car. The wife waited near the front door with a toddler beside her and a baby in her arms.

The man went back inside and the wife turned to go after him. As soon as her back was turned one of the hood rats was there on his bike, snatching a chilly bin from the rear of the wagon. He was gone in a flash, balancing the bin on his handlebars with practiced ease as he pedalled away. His mates followed him and the man came out with another load, oblivious to what had just happened.

'We need to watch our backs,' Gemma said.

They moved off, their heads on swivels as they trotted across the road and left, away from where the group of hood rats on bikes had gone. Alex led the way into a side street a few hundred metres later, then into a short cul-de-sac off that. The street was quiet, the street lights were out and most of the houses seemed to be shut up.

Somebody had been there though, because there was broken glass in the street and a Honda CRV parked at the kerb had been smashed up. Gemma wondered where all the residents were; maybe they had bugged out, or maybe they were laying low inside.

Alex headed to a single storey brick home with a neat garden and a red front door. He took keys from his pocket and turned to Gemma as he unlocked it.

'This is us,' he said, his voice catching. 'I hope Mum's okay.'

Gemma nodded and followed him into a darkened hallway. The house was completely silent and felt empty. The air smelt like it hadn't moved for a couple of days.

Back at the mouth to the cul-de-sac, unbeknown to Gemma and Alex, Cody and Dice watched them enter the house.

While Alex went through the house, calling for his mother, Gemma waited in the lounge at the front. It was a nice tidy house and Alex's mother obviously had a taste for knick-knacks and Lladro china. She moved softly to a side table laden with photographs – Alex at school, Alex graduating from university, Alex and his mum in a restaurant, Alex and a bunch of similarly-geeky-looking mates.

No dad, no siblings, no girlfriends. She shrugged mentally and turned as he came back.

'She's not here,' he said, 'looks like she hasn't even been home.'

'Is her car here?'

'No.'

Gemma nodded. They stood in the silence for a few moments. Gemma could feel Alex's anxiety and she sympathised. She knew that his mum worked as a medical receptionist in Hillsborough. It didn't surprise her that she hadn't made it home yet. With any luck she was hunkered down at work or at a friend's place.

'It's nearly dark,' she said. 'I think we should stay here the night. Maybe she'll get home in the morning.'

'Maybe.' Alex's voice was heavy.

'I need to leave in the morning though,' Gemma said carefully. She didn't want to add to the stress she knew he would already be feeling, but he needed to know her intentions. She'd always been clear on that.

She needed to get home.

43

I heard them coming before I saw them.

They had their headlights off but the piece of shit cars they drove gave the game away before they'd even got to our road. One had a rattley exhaust and the other was a V8 that hadn't been tuned since the turn of the century.

I was outside already, checking that our own vehicles were locked and secure. Archie was asleep inside and the oldies were getting ready for bed. Jethro had been out for a crap and gone back inside to sleep outside Archie's door. I had intended to stay up longer and take a patrol of our property. I was so wired I knew I wouldn't be sleeping any time soon anyway.

The Rossi was in my hands and the Ruger GP100 was holstered on my hip. I felt like a sheriff in the Wild West. Hearing the cars approaching, I knew with absolute certainty that shit was about to go down. There hadn't been a single car go down our road all day. For two to arrive together once night had fallen meant only one thing.

Whoever was driving the vehicles obviously had no tactical training. Brake lights flared as they slid to a stop near the end of our driveway, lighting up the road nice and red. I was at the side door already, calling urgently to Rob. He came hurrying out, buckling up his jeans as he did so.

'We've got visitors,' I said in a low voice. 'Get your gun and look after these guys. Keep Jethro inside.'

'Who is it?'

'I'd say the same guys from last night.'

'Where're you going?'

I worked the lever on the Rossi. 'I'm gunna stop the fuckers.'

With that I moved off, hearing the cars starting to move. I crossed the parking area to the other side, away from the house. I doubted they had any night vision capability, and the house would be their focus. The ammo belt around my waist carried spare .357 Magnum rounds which could be used in either weapon, and I had more in my pockets.

These pricks had made a bad call coming back.

I leaned in against the post and rail fence to the right of the drive-way, hearing the rumble of the engines and the crunch of the gravel under the approaching tyres.

I let them get half way up the driveway before I fired the first shot. This was not the time for warnings, nor was it the time to fuck about. They had signalled their intent with their almost-stealthy approach, and I couldn't afford to let them get close enough to harm my family.

The bullet cracked the windscreen of the lead vehicle, which was an old Ford Fairmont, and the car came to an immediate stop. The one behind it crashed into its rear and nudged it forward before both vehicles stopped. I could hear shouts inside the cars.

I chambered a fresh round and sighted on the glass right in front of the driver. I knew the windscreen would be much weaker now, and the second shot should nail the driver. Luckily for him he opened his door and debussed. Unluckily for him the second driver chose that second to hit his headlights, lighting up the front car like a Christmas tree.

The driver had a long weapon of some sort in his hands and the front passenger was also carrying what looked like a rifle.

I didn't hesitate. The second round punched through the passenger's window, showering him with glass and dropping him like a screaming stone. I crabbed along to my left, working the lever, and took a bead on the driver. He was standing there gaping like a fish, unable to comprehend what had just happened.

My third shot pulled slightly right and skimmed across his shoulder, spinning him into the side of the car. I could hear screaming and shouting above the humming in my ears. The second car started racing back down the driveway, and its headlights showed me that there were two more heads in the back of the lead car. Wisely, they had stayed put.

Using the fence as a shooting platform, I put a round into the front grill of the retreating second car. It wobbled but carried on, and I gave it a second round. That bullet shattered the left headlight and it went dark. In the partial light I recognised it as a crappy Subaru with primer paint. The driver hit the gas and careened down the drive. He did well not to veer off into the fence either side, but he overshot and went straight across the road into the ditch opposite.

I left them to it and turned back to the guys in the Ford. The driver was still screaming and propping himself up against the door. I couldn't see the front passenger but I could hear him, whimpering and groaning. The rear doors were open now and I could see one dark figure at the back of the car, another off to the side. It was too dark to see any weapons, but I was treating them all as armed and out to kill. I gave myself a mental uppercut for not having any night vision kit.

My mind racing for the next move, I was scanning for targets when I saw movement from the rear of the car. One of the passengers came around and hustled the wounded driver into the back seat, slammed the door, and got behind the wheel. He revved the engine and ground the gears and lurched forward. The headlights came on and lit up the whole drive and turning area.

I was shifting my aim across to my right, looking for the other rear passenger, when I caught movement off to the left. It was the guy I was looking for and he had picked up the driver's discarded weapon.

The weapon was swinging towards me and I came back to get a bead. He knew I was there and he wanted me.

A heavy shot boomed out from the house and the guy dropped.

The Fairmont revved, the taillights came on and it started backwards. The fallen front passenger was down on his side, not moving. The Fairmont kept going, leaving him where he was. I shifted to my left, taking the risk of exposing myself to push the point home. I heard my last round ping off the bodywork somewhere and I stepped back into the shadows, reloading as fast as my fumbling fingers would go.

'Mark!' Rob came from the back door with his rifle in his hands. 'I shot the bastard!'

Jethro came with him, barking excitedly.

'I saw,' I said. My ears were ringing so much it made my voice sound disembodied. 'Thanks. I'm going after them.'

'They're gone.'

'Not far enough. You stay up here and cover me.'

I jumped the fence and set off at a trot towards the road. Jethro came with me, a comforting figure darting about in the dark. The Fairmont had swung around and was idling on the road while a bustle of activity took place at the Subaru. Dark figures were heaving it out of the ditch and there was frantic shouting and swearing. They were panicking and I felt myself smile. They were going to get the good news and some.

I hung back from the fence, keeping myself in the dark and assessing what was going on. One guy was standing guard with a rifle and another guy was pacing round with a baseball bat. From what I could see most of them were guys with just a couple of girls, a range of ages and all were scruffy looking thugs.

I had no doubt they were related to the clowns I'd chased off the previous night, and if they thought they could come here and intimidate me, they were sorely mistaken.

The Subaru was up on the road now and they were starting to get themselves sorted. There was still lots of chaotic shouting and arm waving, until one older guy told them all to shut up and listen.

'Get in the fuckin' cars,' he said, 'we gotta get some help for that boy. Where's Kayden, where's he at?'

'He got fuckin' shot, man,' one of the girls wailed. 'They just shot that nigger down, man. He's dead!'

The older guy cursed, paced for a few seconds, then waved his hands for silence. 'Shut the fuck up,' he said. 'Ain't nothin' we can do 'bout that now. Get home and I'll come up with a better plan.' He turned towards my house and shouted into the darkness. 'We comin' back, bitches! Gonna fuck you up!'

My voice cut through the few whoops he got.

'You cunts come back here,' I said, 'and I'll kill the fuckin' lot of you.'

'Jesus fuck!' The older man jumped with fright and a couple of them ducked for cover.

The guy with the rifle turned in my direction, bringing his weapon around. The crack of the Rossi was loud and he dropped with a bullet in his chest. I moved offline, keeping a bead on them.

'Get him in your car and fuck off,' I called out. 'You got ten seconds before I start shooting you one by one.'

They began to move, the older man and another guy grabbing the gunner I'd just dropped and pulling him towards the Fairmont. Someone else went to pick up his gun.

'Leave it,' I said.

The guy paused with his hand over it, searching for me in the dark.

'Touch it and I'll kill you.'

He backed away and I became aware of a strange dragging sound coming from my left. I looked that way and spotted Rob as he reached the roadside. He dropped something and stepped away from it.

'Come and pick up your shit before you go,' he called out, his voice wheezy.

The older man and his mate got the gunner into the car and hurried over. In the ambient light from the headlights I saw them grab up a fallen figure, slinging his arms over their shoulders.

'You fuckin' shoot him, old man?' the older guy said, a hint of menace in his voice.

'Yeah I did.' Rob's tone left no room for argument. 'And I'll shoot you too if you don't hurry up.'

They muttered and cursed but they got him to the car too. Everyone else was already in and waiting for them. I could hear crying and groaning from them.

'Remember what I said. Come back here, any of you, anywhere near here, and we'll kill the whole fuckin' lot of you. You had your chance.'

'We never had a chance,' the older guy spat. 'You just shot us down like dogs. Is that all we are to you?'

'You called it. Your boys walked away yesterday; they should've stayed away. You came back here trying to hurt us, and you lost. Don't try again.'

'Or what?' He was surprisingly defiant for someone who's gang had just been ass-kicked. The belligerence of these types of people never ceased to amaze me.

'You don't have enough body bags,' I told him. 'Now go.'

He cursed again but got behind the wheel of the Subaru and slammed the door. He leaned out the window as the car started to move off.

'This ain't over, cunt,' he called out.

I punched a shot through the open window into his windscreen. Someone screamed and both cars took off.

We waited a few moments to be sure they'd gone.

'You okay?' Rob called out.

'Yep, you?'

'Yep.'

I joined him at the fence.

'Think they'll be back?' he said.

I reached down and scratched Jethro's head. 'I hope not. But we've got plenty of ammo if they do.'

Looking down the road where I'd last seen them, I caught the slightest glimpse of movement in the darkness. Wishing again that I had some NVGs, I squinted for a better look. It was on the shoulder of the road outside Bevan's house, a good way down, and it was just a shift of darkness within the shadows. Like a person moving back from the road towards their house.

'Bevan,' I whispered to myself. I could picture him down there in the dark with his rifle in his hands, ready to go.

It wasn't a comforting thought.

44

Dawn was breaking when Gemma got up. She'd had a fitful sleep in the spare room, the strange surroundings adding to the stress of the day before.

They had been late to bed the night before. Alex had skinned his elbow and knee when he'd fallen earlier, and Gemma had cleaned and patched his grazes. They had found lasagne in the fridge, leftover from dinner three nights ago. They had shared it, eating ravenously, neither having realised how hungry they were.

They had sat in the darkened lounge and talked, processing the events of the last couple of days and planning ahead as best they could. Alex wasn't sure whether to hunker down at home and wait for his mum, or to go with Gemma.

'That's a decision for you,' she had told him. 'You're welcome to come with me if you like, but I understand.'

It clearly bothered him that she had killed a man, probably two, and he queried her on it.

'How did it feel?' he had asked. 'Were you...scared?'

It was a fair question, even though it felt raw. Gemma had taken some time to consider her response.

'I was shitting myself both times,' she said honestly. 'Especially the first, with the cops...they would have killed us.' She had felt a surge of emotion as she spoke, a wave of anger at the thugs who had attacked them. It was so strong that she felt her hands tremble. 'I had to. I had no choice.'

Alex nodded slowly in the darkness, and his next words caught her by surprise.

'Thank you,' said quietly. 'I'm glad you were there.'

She had dreamed again of killing people, but this time the snatches she could remember were accompanied by a feeling of power. She had saved their lives again, of that she had no doubt. Firstly with the mob down by the lagoon, then again with the family of boguns and their mongrel dog.

Shaking off the tiredness, she had dressed quickly – the same clothes she'd been wearing since hitting the road – and got down on the floor for some stretches. The constant walking and running and carrying a bag, along with sleeping on the ground the night before, had given her legs and shoulders in particular a hammering. Her joints groaned and clicked but after some stretching and deep breathing, she felt looser and ready to go.

Gemma had slept with the Glock beside her and she checked it again, despite having checked it last night. She had removed the partially spent magazine, which now had eleven rounds, and replaced it with a full one of seventeen. She knew that twenty-eight rounds wouldn't last long if things really went bad, but it was all she had. Hopefully she wouldn't need a single round before she got home, let alone all twenty-eight.

She packed her gear and padded to the kitchen. Even though the power was off the fridge had remained cool, and she found milk and yoghurt in there. She found a can of peaches in the pantry. She poured herself a bowl of bran and sultana cereal, added the peaches and dairy and stepped into the dining room.

Alex sat at the table with a sandwich on a plate in front of him, staring out the window. Gemma jumped when she saw him sitting in the darkness.

'Sorry,' he said, 'couldn't sleep. I've been up since four.'

Gemma sat and started on her breakfast. 'How're you feeling?'

He shrugged. 'I dunno really.' He pushed a piece of paper across to her. 'I'm gunna leave this for my mum.'

Gemma read the note as she ate. He was telling his mother that he was going with his workmate to her house and that he hoped she would be safe. He told her he would be in contact as soon as he could, but he didn't feel safe staying at home to wait for her.

'Is that okay?' Alex's eyes were tired but hopeful.

'Of course.' Gemma finished her mouthful. 'I'd feel safer having you with me.'

'Seriously?'

'Seriously.'

He nodded and almost smiled. She could see the relief in his face.

'We need to get going though,' Gemma said. 'We can eat, clean up a bit and see if there's any food or anything here that we could use. It'd be great if we could get a car or some bikes, but it may not happen.'

They finished their breakfast in silence before going through the kitchen cupboards. The problem they had was space – they didn't have enough room to take too much. Gemma had hoped to find proper packs, but Alex and his mother had nothing in the way of camping gear. She chose to not use the carry bags they did have – yesterday had driven home the need to keep her hands free. They would have to make do with what they had.

'Eat up,' Gemma said. 'We eat as much as we can now and we take some with us. With any luck we'll be home today. If we get a car we could be home in about an hour.'

They topped up their bags with high-energy food – muesli bars, biscuits, chocolate, and dried fruit. They each downed a couple of small bottles of water flavoured with orange and mango, the sugar giving them an instant hit. Gemma crammed the rest of the bag of bran and sultana cereal into her bag and Alex took some matches, a tin of baked beans and some peanut butter sandwiches wrapped in clingfilm.

While Alex went and sorted out his clothes, Gemma took the

opportunity to use the toilet with actual toilet paper. The toilet flushed once and didn't refill, but the relief was immense. It was almost like being normal again.

Alex appeared in the lounge with his bag, dressed now in cotton cargo pants, his own sneakers and a comfortable shirt. He hefted his bag onto his back.

'I hope she'll be okay,' he said.

'I'm sure she will.' Gemma tried to sound upbeat, but she really just wanted to get going. 'Come on, before everyone's up and about.'

45

A s the sun came up, I sat on the deck with a cup of steaming coffee in my hand.

I was warm in my jacket, jeans and boots. I wore a beanie and a three-day growth. Jethro sat beside me and I idly scratched his head. The Rossi leaned against the deck railing and Pepper sat on the top rail above it, surveying her kingdom.

I had cleaned up the bullet casings and broken plastic from the driveway. Archie had somehow slept through the whole thing, but we had had a late night with the ladies, talking through what had happened. They were understandably concerned, so Rob and Sandy had come in from the motorhome and taken our room. Rob and I had cracked a bottle of Glenfiddich and shared a decent dram.

I had spent the rest of the night on the couch with one eye open.

Light footsteps sounded behind me and Archie appeared, greeting the day with a smile. He'd always been an early riser. He wore Batman slippers and rocket ship pyjamas, no dressing gown despite the early chill. He came to me for a cuddle and I kissed his soft cheek.

'Morning, Dad.'

'Morning, wee man.'

He climbed onto my lap and snuggled in against the cold of the morning. I held him and watched the dawn light slowly spread across the horizon. The clouds were clear and it was shaping up to be a decent day.

Forty-eight hours had passed since the national state of emergency had been declared. Considering what had happened in that short space of time, things weren't going to improve in the short term. My suspicions were confirmed a moment later when Rob stepped out onto the deck. He had bare feet and a sweater hastily thrown on over his pyjamas.

His transistor radio was in his hand and I could hear an announcer's voice.

I looked at him quizzically. His eyes were wide and his lips were tight.

'What is it?'

He held the radio up as he came over.

'...so that's just in from the Beehive, the Prime Minister has declared a state of martial law, effective immediately. A formal statement will follow shortly, but the breaking news is that martial law is now in effect in New Zealand for the first time in history...'

I locked eyes with Rob, a jolt of cold electricity running through my body. An unspoken fear passed between us.

I wrapped my arm across Archie's small frame and held him close. Things were about to get worse and we needed to be ready for it.

The third day was just beginning.

BONUS CHAPTERS

EARLY WARNING SERIES #2

GETTING HOME

The chill of the autumn night was easing now that Curtis was on his second smoke.

The first had been a cigarette, a starter to get the day going, and the second was a point of meth that he shared with his wife, Lena.

The buzz of the P – pure methamphetamine – got his senses pinging and staved off the chill.

He shifted the Beretta semi-auto in his lap, feeling the weight of it. It was a 1301 Tactical in 12-gauge, traded some years back for meth. The extended tubular magazine gave it a 6-round capacity plus one in the chamber, which Curtis always took advantage of.

Lena eyed him as his fingers stroked the receiver and came to rest on the trigger guard.

'You love that fuckin' gun,' she said.

Curtis crooked a smile at her. 'Yes I fuckin' do,' he agreed.

The glint in his eye unnerved Lena. Years ago he had looked at her with desire like that. The only thing he seemed to desire these days was guns and crack.

He saw their niece, Shavaunne, approaching on foot. Behind her was the mouth of a quiet residential cul-de-sac. They were parked in The Gardens, the "first class" part of Manurewa. He knew the cul-de-sac was quiet because they had been parked in the truck – a red and silver Ford F150 – for the last two hours. Dawn had broken in that time.

Shavaunne and her brother Dice, the big lump of psycho, had been watching a house all night. In that house were a man and a woman, and today they were going to die.

The previous afternoon, the woman had shot and killed Shavaunne's other brother, Jaysin, and his dog, who was only known as Bastard.

Curtis cracked his window as Shavaunne approached.

'Still there,' Shavaunne said without preamble. She was shivering and wiped her nose on the sleeve of her hoody. She looked like she needed a hit.

'Any movement?'

'They're up,' Shavaunne said, eyeing the small glass meth pipe still in Lena's hand. She sniffed the fumes wafting from the truck, desperate for a taste after a night of watching.

'Where's Dice?'

'In the car.'

'He good to go?'

Shavaunne grunted, her eyes on the pipe.

'You deaf, cunt?' Curtis' tone was sharp. 'He good to go?'

'Yeah, fuck, 'course he is. Fuck man, it's cold as shit out here.'

'You want some?' Curtis dug out his tobacco tin, which he always carried. He opened it to show her the gram bag inside and she practically started drooling.

'Yeah, fuck man, I want some. Fuck yeah.'

She reached through the window for it and Curtis gave her the eye. She withdrew her hand quickly. He reached under the car seat and produced a sawn-off over/under shotgun. The butt had been removed to leave just the pistol grip and the twin barrels were no longer than six inches. It was a .410 that he had taken off a dealer.

Shavaunne's eyes gleamed as she took the gun and a handful of spare shells.

'Go cover the back and we'll go in the front,' Curtis said.

Shavaunne nodded and went to step away, but Curtis grabbed her thin wrist. He ignored the anger that flared in her eyes – Shavaunne didn't like being grabbed.

'Remember,' he said, 'they killed your brother.'

She hissed like a cat and jerked her arm away. Curtis turned to Lena.

'Let's go.'

CHASE INVESTIGATIONS SERIES #1
OLD FRIENDS

The depot was quiet and still at 1am on a Monday, a light breeze flicking the odd leaf or piece of rubbish across the forecourt where the trucks came in and turned round to be loaded.

A row of semis lined one side of the compound, big and dark and empty, all emblazoned with Marcus Haulage markings. A security light flickered weakly and cast only a slight glow through the darkness. The chain link fence rattled and the gate squeaked as it was pushed open.

The man at the gate checked his watch nervously for the fourth time in as many minutes. He shivered even though it wasn't cold.

An engine could be heard and a second later bright headlights swept round the corner into the street and approached the end of the cul-de-sac where the man waited on the footpath by the open gate. It was an industrial area populated by trade centres and auto businesses and nobody was around at this time of night.

The lights blinded him as the truck swung easily through the gate and entered the depot, making a wide half circle before smoothly backing up to the loading bay. This wasn't a semi-truck like the ones parked up in a row at the side of the depot, but a smaller delivery truck with no markings. The man shut the gates and looped the chain through without locking it. He hurried over to the truck and met the driver and his passenger as they jumped down.

'Good work,' the driver told him with a smirk, 'let's get to it.'

He was a burly man with greasy hair showing under his cap. He had the strong forearms built from years of guiding 18-wheelers down the highways and the red nose of a hardened drinker. His companion was of a similar build but taller, with tattoos discolouring his own forearms. He also had a spider's web tattooed on the left side of his neck and several tear drops inked into the skin by his right eye. He was harder looking than the driver and didn't speak.

'Hurry,' the man who'd opened the gate said, checking his watch again, and the driver sneered at him with contempt.

'Just open up, fella,' he replied, hitching his jeans up, 'let us do our job.'

The first man unlocked the door beside the loading bay then lifted the roller door. He stood and watched as the other two men entered the warehouse, turned a couple of lights on and got to work. Within twenty minutes they had loaded the back of the truck with several pallets of boxes, replaced the forklift, turned out the lights and locked up again. It was a smooth, efficient operation, done with minimal fuss.

The driver and his companion climbed back into the truck and the nervous man went to the gate to let them out. The truck paused in the gateway and the driver wound down the window, leaning casually out.

'Cheers buddy,' he smirked, 'see ya next time. We'll be in touch, aye?'

The passenger stared at the nervous man with a blank expression, and the nervous man nodded glumly.

'Okay, okay,' he replied, 'just go. Just go.'

The driver laughed and the truck moved away up the road. The nervous man wiped his brow on the sleeve of his jacket, locked the gate again and hurried away into the darkness.

Silence returned to the depot.

The lady sitting on the red fabric sofa in the corner of the office was well dressed and smelt of expensive perfume. She appeared uncomfortable, as if she were waiting for the dentist or a mammogram. She was middle aged and had perfectly styled hair and flawless make up.

The man sitting on the matching chair at right angles to her was twenty years younger, with broad shoulders and a confident air about him. He had dark eyes and dark hair with a hint of grey at the temples, a full moustache, and was dressed in casual chinos and an open necked shirt.

He looked up from the notes he'd made on the pad on his knee and smiled at her. It was a calm reassuring smile, and it eased her discomfort a degree or two. He had a direct gaze and intelligent eyes, the sort of face that was more interesting than handsome. A faint scar showed at his chin, a patch where no stubble could grow.

'Okay Mrs MacNamara,' he said, 'is there anything else you can tell me that may help? Any particular routine that your husband follows that may help me narrow it down a bit?'

She thought for a moment.

'He plays squash every Monday and Thursday night right after work. He always starts work by seven and usually gets home about six.' She frowned. 'That's it I'm afraid. I can't think of anything else.'

'No problem.' He jotted it down, got the name of the squash club from her, and smiled again. 'That's it, Mrs MacNamara. We'll get onto it right away, and give you an update as soon as we know anything, okay?'

'How long will it take?' she asked, and for the first time her voice quavered. She paused to re-gather herself before continuing. 'I mean, will I hear from you this week?'

'It really depends on what your husband does and what we find, Mrs MacNamara.'

He stood and she followed suit, allowing herself to be ushered over to the desk by the door. 'We'll be in touch as soon as we can, hopefully in the next few days.'

She nodded and he gave her that reassuring smile again.

'If you can give your deposit to Molly I'll quickly print off a contract for you.'

He moved to the second desk in the office, which faced the first one across the floor space. Mrs MacNamara turned to the woman at the first desk-Molly-and passed her a gold Visa.

Molly took it and used it to take an electronic deposit of ten hours work. She was a striking woman of classical beauty, with wavy dark hair and sparkling, friendly green eyes. She had full red lips and wore little make up-mainly because she didn't need to. She had the sort of look that defied pigeonholing. She could pass for a European or a country girl, depending on what she wore. Today she wore a simple black skirt and silver blouse, elegant and understated.

Mrs MacNamara cast a furtive look at the man as he printed out a contract for her. He seemed like a nice person but she sensed he was not the sort to mess with. She glanced back at Molly, who was smiling at her and holding her card and receipt out for her. Her eyes smiled as well as her mouth, and Mrs MacNamara felt herself smile in return.

The man came over and gave her a copy of the contract and had her sign his copy. She folded it and put it in her bag with her card and receipt. Then he handed her a business card and smiled again. Molly smiled again too, and Mrs MacNamara felt a little better. She thanked them and allowed him to hold the door for her.

'We'll be in touch,' he told her, and closed the door behind her.

Mrs MacNamara walked towards the stairs down to the street. She could hear the motorway behind her on the other side of the building, and the main street of Ellerslie village was in front of her. She looked at the card in her hand.

Chase Investigations, it said. Dan Crowley, Director. It was a plain white card with blue lettering, the company's name in italicised lettering across the top as if it really was chasing something, his name and title below it in smaller letters. Address and contact details at the bottom.

She tucked it into her bag with the rest of the stuff, and checked her watch. It was 930am. Nearly time for her manicure.

Dan Crowley passed the notes and contract to his wife and went to the kitchenette off the office.

'What do you think?' he asked as he poured a coffee for himself and a green tea for her. 'If we could get a few more Mrs MacNamaras in here with their Remuera cheque books, I'd be happy.'

'If we get a few more Mrs MacNamaras in here, 'Molly replied, 'there won't be room to move. You've got a full week already, honey, and now this as well.'

'I'll give it to old Neil,' he told her, handing her a tea cup and perching on the corner of her desk.

'He's already got a full week as well.' She clicked open the weekly planner on her desktop and opened up the tab for Neil. 'He's in court for the Shelby theft case today, he's got the Parker and Philips fraud, four accident reports due in and he's got five processes.' She took a sip of tea and gave him a plaintive look. 'What, no biscuits this morning?'

Dan went to the kitchenette and brought back the cookie jar.

'How about you, could you squeeze it in?' He bit into a ginger crunch and showered crumbs down his front. He didn't seem to notice.

'I'll have to, won't I?' Molly sighed and frowned at him. He didn't seem to notice that either.

'We need to take someone else on though, honey. Neil's as slow as a wet week.'

'He is officially retired.'

'So he should retire properly then. I'm supposed to be part time but I'm practically full time and you did sixty hours last week.' She pouted at him. 'You need to get someone in.'

He sipped his coffee and nodded.

'You're right.' He smiled at her and patted her cheek affectionately. 'No worries gorgeous, I'll sort it out. I'll talk to Buck and see if he knows of anyone wanting to get out.'

The door opened and an elderly man with grey hair and a beer pot entered, a battered briefcase in one hand and a copy of the Racing Times in the other.

'Morning all,' he said cordially, kicking the door closed behind him, 'how are we?'

'We be fine,' Dan replied with an amused smile. 'How are ye?'

'Ye be good,' Neil replied, taking a seat at the third desk, the one in the corner with the empty file tray. He opened his briefcase and removed a thick manila folder. He carried it over to Molly's desk and put it down with a flourish.

'Here you go, my dear lady,' he said grandly, shooting the cuffs of his dark suit and smoothing his tie. 'All my files, up to date and complete.'

He looked across at Dan, who was coming from the kitchenette with a coffee for him.

'I'm retiring,' he announced, drinking in their surprised looks. 'Yep, I thought it was about time. I don't need to work; I've got my pension and not long left to spend it. June's found a place in Tauranga and put an offer in, it got accepted over the weekend and we move this week.'

'That soon?' Molly looked stunned.

'That soon,' he said. 'I'm sorry to drop it on you like this, but we got the word on Friday night. I cleaned up my files over the weekend, all the documents are served, the crash reports are done and photos on the disk, and I've done the preliminary work on the Parker and Philips job.' He glanced back to Dan. 'You'll just need to finish it off, Daniel.'

'Uh-huh.' Dan nodded and went to his desk. 'You're still in court today, I take it?'

'Indeed, indeed. The last time I'll be giving evidence, I should imagine.' He nodded solemnly. 'No more running round playing private eye for old Neil, it's time for fishing and golf.'

'And spending quality time with June,' Molly reminded him.

'Yeah, that too,' he conceded.

There was an awkward silence for a moment. Nobody seemed to

know what to say. Molly looked to her husband, but he remained silent. She felt her cheeks flush.

'Anyway, I better get to court,' Neil said eventually, 'justice waits for no man.'

'I think you mean time,' Dan told him.

'Don't I know it.'

Neil grabbed his briefcase, took a quick slurp of coffee and was gone, banging the door behind him again as he left.

Dan and Molly looked across the office at each other.

'Be careful what you wish for,' he said.

'D'you think he heard me?' she frowned.

'Probably.' He groaned and rubbed his face. 'Now we really need someone. Better book dinner for four at Luigi's, I guess.'

'Ooh, are you taking your wife out for dinner?' she cooed, making eyes at him across the room.

'Hmm, something like that.' He grinned. 'In company, of course, so you don't get any fancy ideas.'

'Typical. Where's the romance gone?'

'He could've given us more notice than a day,' Dan grumbled. He leaned back in his chair and put his feet up on the edge of the desk.

'That's what you get for taking on a contractor,' she told him, 'all care, no responsibility. I think we should take on a permanent employee this time.'

'Then I'd have to pay them holidays and sick and whatever else they can think of.' He shook his head in despair. 'Just can't get the staff.'

'You've gotta try first. What about Buck?'

'What, Buck himself? Na, he's got it too cushy where he is, why would he give that up?'

'Being the Ellerslie community cop can hardly be stimulating,' Molly opined.

'Not too taxing either, though. He hasn't got himself in trouble since...well...'

'Since he stopped working with you?'

'Exactly.'

His mobile bleeped on the desk with an incoming message. He smiled as he checked it.

'Mike,' he said, 'wants to meet for a coffee urgently.'

'Wonder who he's in love with now?' Molly speculated.

'You're such a cynic.'

'You know it's true. Ten to one it's a drama about some woman.' She gave him a challenging look. 'Go on, bet against me.'

Dan shook his head and got up.

'That's a sucker's bet.' He bent over her desk and kissed her softly on the cheek. 'And I'm no sucker.'

'No, you're a hot shot private eye.' Her eyes twinkled at him. 'But you know what it'll be.'

'Maybe.' He kissed her firmly on the mouth now. 'I'll shoot down and see Buck first, then go see him then head off and do the Parker and Philips case.'

'Hey.' Molly caught him by the sleeve. 'Maybe Mike wants a job?'

'You think?' He considered it for a second then shook his head. 'Na, can you really see him as a PI? Doubt it. We don't do debt collection.'

'You used to,' she reminded him, and he shrugged.

'Yeah, but now we're chasing better money than that. Any port in a storm I guess, but I'd rather Mrs MacNamara brought her friends to see us. At least you know you won't get your head stoved in investigating a cheating husband or corporate fraud.'

He leaned down and kissed her again.

'I'll call you later.'

He left the office, wondering what it was that Mike had got himself into now.

MESSAGE FROM THE AUTHOR

Thanks for taking the time to read *Martial Law*. I hope you enjoyed the first book in the **Early Warning** series. The second book in the series is *Getting Home* - The city is burning and panic has set in. Martial law has brought the military onto the streets to maintain law and order, but the thugs aren't the only threat...

I'd love it if you could please take the time to leave an online review of *Martial Law* with your favourite book retailer.

If you'd like to know about new releases and receive a free book, sign up to my **Hitlist** on Facebook -

https://www.facebook.com/writer-angus-mclean

Cheers,
Angus McLean

ACKNOWLEDGMENTS

The author would like to thank the advisers who have assisted with the writing of this book. They must remain anonymous for security reasons, but they (and only they) know who they are.

They are the true heroes who put their lives on the line to protect our freedoms. My sincerest gratitude goes out to them.

And once again, huge thanks to "Tori" who does my covers and provides great advice. You rock.

This is a work of fiction, and all errors are the responsibility of the author.

ABOUT THE AUTHOR

Angus McLean is a South Auckland Police officer.

His experience as a cop and a private investigator give his writing a touch of realism. He believes reading should be escapist entertainment and is inspired by the TV shows he watched as a youngster.

His real identity remains a secret.

www.writerangusmclean.com

www.ingramcontent.com/pod-product-compliance
Lightning Source LLC
Chambersburg PA
CBHW070602120726
47909CB00007B/2414